Just One More
Temptation

The Sterling Family
Book 4

NEW YORK TIMES BESTSELLING AUTHOR
Carly Phillips

JUST ONE MORE TEMPTATION

He's a grumpy single dad who's serious and uptight.
She's a younger free spirit who's sunshine and light.

Fallon Sterling's one experience with a rich, older man ended in heartbreak. So when twin nine-year-old girls wind up in her gallery, followed by their oh-so-hot dad, she refuses to notice how sexy he is. And she will not let herself fall for his broody charms. Or his adorable daughters. That *was* her plan. Unfortunately, planning hasn't always been her strong suit...

Noah Powers needs a reliable nanny, *not* a romance with a much younger artist who his girls adore. The fact that he desires Fallon and the sunshine she brings into his drab world doesn't matter. His focus needs to be on his work and his daughters. Trouble is, he can never remember that when Fallon is in his arms.

Somewhere between a matchmaking family (his) and dangerous workplace drama (hers), Fallon and Noah realize they might have more in common than they thought. But is it enough for happily ever after?

Just One More Temptation, book 4 in the stand-alone Sterling Family series, is a spicy, fun, hot, age-gap, single-dad, contemporary romance. Welcome to romantic escapism at its steamiest.

Dear Reader:

As occasionally happens, I discovered that I made a consistency error in this book. In *Just One More Moment* and *Just One More Dare*, Fallon Sterling owned a gallery. In this book, Clara Morganville owns the gallery where Fallon works. To readers who have read the prior books, I will be making changes in the earlier stories to be consistent with this one. To new readers, don't worry about a thing. Just read and enjoy.

All the best,
Carly (who is only human!)

Chapter One

N OAH POWERS FRANTICALLY searched the New York City park for his twin nine-year-old girls, calling their names, ignoring the looks from the mothers with their younger children playing in the sandbox. He turned to Hazel, the sixty-year-old woman he'd hired when their last nanny had been too young and flighty to keep an eye on his girls. They'd been acting out lately but they'd never run away. Hadn't he lectured them enough about stranger danger and staying with an adult?

"Dammit!" he yelled, pulling his hand through his hair.

"I'm so sorry, Mr. Powers. I was watching them, I swear. They asked if they could go to the pretzel truck on the corner and I had an eye on them. I blinked and they disappeared."

He ground his teeth together. "Because you didn't go with them."

She looked down, not answering since he was right.

"You stay here in case they come back." He strode toward the cart and questioned the man selling food who said he'd sold them a pretzel and soda but didn't see the direction they went after.

Panicked, Noah rushed down the sidewalk, scanning inside each shop and walking into the larger ones. Heart in his throat, he looked in each window, not seeing their brown-haired heads.

He swallowed hard and a horrific thought ran through his head. What if someone had taken them? No. They were just being difficult because they hadn't liked Hazel from the moment he'd hired her. Then again, it was the same story with every nanny no matter their age. They missed their mother and there was nothing he could do to change the fact that Charlie, an archaeologist, had been invited on the dig of her dreams.

They'd shared custody until six months ago. For all their lives, she'd had the girls during the week and he'd taken them one night a weekday and every other weekend. Despite the explanation, they'd hoped their mom would be home by now but the dig was long. Even with Charlie coming home to see them often, it wasn't the same as their mom being here. Noah was doing the best he could on his own but his kids were disappointed and too damn smart for their own good.

One thing he knew, when he found them, they'd be grounded for life. And he would find them. There was no acceptable alternative.

FALLON STERLING WALKED to the front of the paint and sip side of the art gallery where she worked, two glass cups of frothy cappuccino in hand. She passed the rectangular table she'd set up for tonight's class, including the easels, paints, brushes, and other materials. Her best friend, Brooklyn Snyder, who she called Brooke for short, had stopped by to say hello and helped her arrange the items since Fallon's usual assistant, Sylvie, was out with a bad cold.

Fallon handed her friend a cappuccino and gestured to two stools by the bar where they usually sold wine and snacks. "Let's sit."

They strode across the room and Fallon took the seat facing inside, a habit so she could look around and make sure she hadn't missed anything that her students would need later.

"Let me run to the ladies' room," Brooke said, grabbing her purse. "Be right back."

Fallon glanced around, her gaze landing on two of her modern, pop art paintings hanging on the walls. The feeling of pride swirling inside her never grew old. Even as a child, she'd loved to work with bright colors. In college, she'd dual majored in art history and fine arts, minoring in business at the Rhode Island School of Design.

Then she'd moved back to New York and worked first at a museum and for the last year and a half, here at the gallery. Her dream was to own a place like this one day but for now, she enjoyed her career and the opportunity to combine the painting she loved with helping the owner with the business.

Brooke returned and settled into the seat beside her. "So? When are you going to get your family in for a session?" She gestured to the easels.

"Do you really think any of my brothers would paint and sip?" Fallon asked, shaking her head, smiling at the thought. She took a taste of the hot froth and savored the cinnamon sprinkled on top, licking her lips to remove any remnants.

Brooke chuckled. "I guess you're right but the image is amusing." And she would know.

Of all Fallon's friends, Brooke knew Fallon's family best since she'd grown up in the gatehouse on the property Fallon's father had purchased. Brooke's mother had been their housekeeper and her father the groundskeeper before he'd passed away. These days, her mom, Lizzie, insisted on keeping her job but she was also seeing Fallon's father and Fallon suspected things were serious between them.

"Only *you* got your mother's talent," Brooke mused.

As always happened at the mention of her mother,

4

a lump rose in her throat, forcing Fallon to swallow over it. Gloria Sterling had been killed at home when Fallon was ten years old.

Pushing that thought away, she replied to Brooke's comment. "I'm glad I inherited something meaningful from her." Something more than a trust fund or jewelry, though Fallon was grateful for all of it.

Brooke put a hand over Fallon's. "I'm sorry. I know that's a pain that will never heal."

"Like your dad is for you." When they were younger, Fallon and Brooke had bonded over their similar losses.

Brooke nodded. "At least you know my mom's keeping a close eye on your father after his heart attack."

With a nod, Fallon said, "I'm so glad they're dating or whatever they call it. Your mom is the best person I know, and I appreciate that she watches out for Dad, correcting his bad eating and work habits. If only he'd listen more."

She and the rest of her siblings were worried their father wasn't paying enough attention to the cardiologist's orders to work less, take it easy, and change his dietary choices. Seeing him weak and in the hospital still haunted Fallon. She was a daddy's girl and didn't mind admitting it. To her, Alex Sterling was larger than life. He was also the only parent she had left and she couldn't lose him. Having Lizzie around to look after him eased all their minds.

"Besides, they both deserve to be happy," Brooke said.

"Agreed." They clinked glasses and sipped their hot drinks.

Brooke tucked a strand of hair behind her ear. "Are you going to see the new band at The Back Door this weekend?" she asked of the bar Fallon's brother, Remy, co-owned with his friend, Zach Dare.

"Wouldn't miss it." Remy and Zach had recently begun bringing in entertainment. It was loud inside the bar but the patrons loved it. "How about you?"

Brooke nodded. "Aiden said he'd try not to work too late and meet me there." One of Fallon's brothers was a foreign correspondent and traveled the world but when their father had his heart attack, he'd done his best to help Jared pick up the slack.

The entry chimes rang and before Fallon turned to see who it was, a young, female voice called out. "Mom!" She yelled the word in an excited, raised tone.

Fallon set her drink down and pivoted toward the door to find two young girls staring, disappointment etched in their identical expressions.

"Oh, no! You're not our mom," one said, her bottom lip quivering. Her brown hair was braided on either side of her head and hung past her shoulders.

The other had her hair pulled back in a ponytail. Besides the different hairstyles, they looked exactly alike.

"Are you two lost?" Fallon asked, rising to her feet.

Beside her, Brooke did the same.

"From behind you look just like our mom," the girl with the braids said, eyeing her with curiosity.

Fallon's hand immediately went to her hair and she laughed. "Nope, I'm not anyone's mother."

The other twin nudged her sister with her elbow. "I told you it couldn't be her. Mom's in Egypt," she said in a sulky voice.

Fallon exchanged worried glances with Brooke. "Girls, are you lost?" she asked again, stepping toward them.

They looked at each other, neither answering.

"Maybe we should call the police? Someone's got to be worried about you," Brooke said.

Nodding, Fallon pulled her phone from a deep pocket in her flowing skirt.

"No! We don't trust the po-po!" the one with braids said, folding her arms across her chest.

It was all Fallon could do not to burst out laughing. "That sounds like a line in a Madea movie. Come on, girls. I'm serious. If your mom is in Egypt, where's your dad?"

Wide-eyed, they stared at each other, obviously catching on that they were going to be in trouble. But neither replied.

"How old are you?" Fallon tried, wanting to guide them into revealing information.

"Nine," they said at the same time.

Still young enough to need a babysitter in New York City.

"Do either of you know your dad's phone number?" She stared them down until the one with the ponytail caved.

"Fine. It's—"

"Hang on," Fallon said, opening her phone and then the keypad. "Go ahead."

She voiced the phone number as Fallon typed it in and hit send, but the call rang once and went to voicemail.

Suddenly, the door swung open and a frazzled, *gorgeous* man stepped inside. His dark hair was tousled, as if he'd been running his fingers through the strands, sensual lips were pulled into a firm line, but there was no denying he was one good-looking specimen.

"Dakota, Dylan, I've been searching all over for you!" their father said in a stern voice but there was no mistaking the relief beneath. "You both have some explaining to do!"

"Uh-oh, we're in tro-u-ble!" the twins said in a

singsong voice.

"And you!" He turned to face Fallon. "Can I ask what you're doing playing on the phone?" He gestured toward her hands that held her cell. "You have two little girls who don't belong here and need your help and you're doing, what? Checking out social media?"

All her warm, fuzzy feelings for the worried man disappeared. Treating him to her fakest smile, she said, "I suggest you check your phone before jumping to conclusions."

He pulled his cell from his pocket and a red flush highlighted his nicely carved cheekbones as he obviously saw a missed call. "I apologize," he muttered. "I didn't hear it ring and since they don't have phones, I didn't think to check."

"Apology accepted. I'm sure you were scared out of your mind." She extended her hand. "I'm Fallon Sterling," she said, deciding names were in order. "I work here. And this is my friend Brooke," she said.

Brooke merely waved. She'd been quiet, watching this entire exchange with interest. No doubt they'd be talking about the sexy man later.

He slid his hand against hers and an electrical kick sizzled up her arm, the jolt of awareness taking her off guard. Good lord, it had been years since she'd experienced anything like that feeling. True, she'd appreciated other men's good looks on sight but this one, with his buttoned shirt rolled up at the sleeves, exuded power, and Fallon was drawn to guys who were sure of themselves. Too bad that kind of man had caused her greatest humiliation and heartbreak. Besides, she thought, he had a wife, even if she was in Egypt.

"Noah Powers," he said, his voice huskier than before. As if he were equally attracted to her.

Something she had to be imagining. Lord knew she'd done it before and learned the hard way she wasn't good at reading people's true intentions.

"I'm a partner at a law office up the street," he said. "As for the girls, their nanny brought them to the park to hang out before she dropped them off with me for dinner and they pulled a disappearing act."

"Because we don't like her!"

"Dakota!" he snapped.

"Daddy, don't be mad," the twin she now figured out was Dylan, said. "We saw the lady from behind and she looked like Mommy." She pointed to Fallon.

Once again, Fallon ran her hand over her hair.

"The girls mentioned your wife is in Egypt," Fallon murmured.

"We're not married but yes, their mother is there on an archaeological dig," he said.

She refused to question why that admission made her so happy.

"Daddy, doesn't she remind you of Mom?" one of the twins asked.

"Goddammit," he muttered, rubbing his chest, and she wondered if he was having a bad case of ingestion thanks to his precocious children. "You two are going to give me a heart attack!"

"Daddy!" Dakota said in a chiding tone. "Please calm down. Stress can affect the body's cardiovascular system and raise your blood pressure and *that* can cause a stroke."

A strangled sound of held-back laughter caught Fallon's attention. She didn't look at Brooke because then she'd be laughing out loud and the girls didn't need any sign of encouragement.

Noah pinched the bridge of his nose and sighed. "Then please try to behave. And *never* run away again. I love you both too much to lose you." The bite in his tone eased with his admission.

And Fallon's heart melted, watching his expression soften as he looked at his girls.

"Dad, check out this painting!" Dylan said loudly, pointing to Fallon's artwork. "I love it! Look at all the colors!"

"I love it too!" Dakota added.

Brooke chuckled. "That's a Fallon Sterling original," her friend said.

"You painted this?" Dylan asked.

Fallon nodded. "Modern pop art," she said, aware of the enthusiasm she always exuded when she discussed her craft. "It's always called to me in the works of Andy Warhol, Robert Rauschenberg, and Roy Lichtenstein. Art is my passion and I could get lost for hours painting or viewing other creators' works."

"Can we buy it? I bet it'd look so cool in our room," Dakota exclaimed.

He shook the head she was sure was about to explode from their precociousness. "Do you two think I'm going to reward you for this stunt?"

Dakota dipped her head. "Sorry, Daddy."

"Sorry, Daddy," Dylan echoed.

They both appeared contrite, but something told Fallon these two would be plotting again at their first opportunity.

"Now apologize to Fallon," Noah said in a stern voice.

Two sets of identical faces glanced at her. "We're sorry, Fallon."

"That's okay," she said, smiling at them.

He nodded, his gaze softening now that the girls had done as he'd asked. "Thanks for looking out for them. They won't bother you again."

She bit her cheek before she could say they weren't a bother. He didn't need her encouraging them to come back, though she definitely enjoyed their humor and different but extroverted personalities.

He extended his arm and she placed her palm in his large hand. Their shake was brief this time but his grip was strong and capable, and she had a sudden vision of those hands running over the most sensitive parts of her body. She trembled at the thought and stepped back, taking him in before he disappeared forever.

His hair was a dark brown with a few strands of gray. She placed him in his mid to late thirties, much older than she was, and she would *not* go down that road again. Too many things about this man reminded her of her professor ex, and her humiliating past. Something she didn't need to worry about since once they walked out that door, she'd never see Noah Powers and his adorable twins again. The thought made her sad.

"Girls, I need to get back to Hazel and tell her I found you. Say goodbye," he said, nodding at her and Brooke.

Dakota and Dylan pouted at the mention of their nanny and she hoped Noah fired the woman for letting the twins run wild in Manhattan.

"Bye!" Dylan and Dakota yelled as they looked back at her.

Fallon waved and they smiled before they strode out, the door closing behind them.

NOAH SAT AT the kitchen table with his girls who ate their spaghetti and meatballs in silence. They knew better than to speak when he was as upset as they'd made him. He'd never been as afraid in his life as when he'd received the panicked call from Hazel that his kids were missing. Hazel, who had quit via text, something he'd discovered when he'd walked out of the gallery and checked his cell.

Thank God he'd found his kids. He should have bought them phones like they'd been asking for, he thought, watching them slurp the pasta strands. Of course, doing it now would be rewarding their little stunt today, but their safety came first. As much as he wanted to punish them, he'd already done some serious reprimanding, Dakota had solemnly stated statistics that backed up his concerns, and they'd apologized.

At least he knew for sure now they'd memorized his cell number, which was a plus. If he hadn't caught sight of them in the gallery window, he'd have eventually seen the call from the young woman who worked there. Fallon, who somehow reminded the girls of their mother, enough to draw them into the shop. He could see the physical resemblance from behind but she looked nothing like Charlie.

Something about Fallon Sterling had stopped him in his tracks. Though he'd found the kids, he'd still been worked up and angry but once he was able to focus, he'd been struck by her beauty. Entranced, even. He'd wanted her immediately and for a man who'd kept his social life to the bare minimum since the girls were born, that was saying something.

"Daddy, did you like the paintings we saw today?" Dylan asked, breaking the silence.

"I don't know. I didn't have time to really look at them." He'd been too busy memorizing Fallon's cute nose and the freckles on her cheeks. But at a glance, the work had been fun and attractive, not that he'd tell that to his troublemakers.

Dakota was his little fact spewer and Dylan was the more pragmatic twin. She'd feel him out and guide him in the direction she wanted him to go. In this case, buying a painting they hadn't even priced. He had a hunch her desire for art involved seeing Fallon again. She'd made as much of an impression on his girls as she had on him. Very different impressions for very different reasons.

Noah had taken one look at her pouty lips and wanted a taste. He'd caught sight of that crinkly flowing skirt and all he could think about was lifting it up, sliding her panties aside, and thrusting his cock inside her. Which had his dick reacting, something that

15

never happened with his kids around. That in itself told him Fallon was dangerous.

"I looked up modern pop art, Daddy, and it includes imagery from popular culture." Dakota put her spoon down. "I'm finished."

He nodded. "Do you even know what popular culture is?"

She wrinkled her nose. "Duh. It's what the modern person finds interesting. Like the Taylor Swift effect. Or those soup labels by the man Fallon told us about. Andy umm…"

"Warhol." So Dakota had done the research. "Okay. The paintings were impressive." He gave in because they'd keep going if he didn't. "But I'm sure they're too expensive."

Noah came from family money that ensured he never had to work but it was important to him to be independent and self-sufficient, and to teach his girls the same values.

Dylan curled a leg beneath her on the chair. "But we could go back and find out the cost."

And there it was. They wanted to see Fallon again.

He couldn't, and not just because of the hazardous attraction he felt for her. She'd talked about her art as a passion, something she felt compelled to follow, her words reminding him of Charlie's when it came to her archaeology. She found her career a passion worth pursuing no matter the cost or collateral damage and Fallon struck him as much the same.

He and Charlie had always been oil and water; his feet on the ground, hers in the clouds on the intangible. They'd had sparks though and a night at an airport hotel during a weather delay, led to the twins. He'd never begrudge her, her career but the way the girls had focused in on Fallon told him how much Charlie's presence was missed.

But that didn't mean Fallon was the woman to fill it. For any of them.

Chapter Two

NOAH HAD SEARCHED and made umpteen calls, and he couldn't find a new nanny. The agency he'd been using had politely suggested he try a different company. Apparently, he was being booted. His girls had run through too many caregivers for him to count. It was Noah's bad luck that it was summertime and they were off from school. He managed easier during the year with a neighbor he'd paid to pick the girls up from school and watch them until he came home around dinnertime.

But now that they were on break, he needed someone full time. Sleepaway camp like some of their friends was off the table. He wanted to make the most of his time with his daughters while he still could. Before they became teenagers and no longer wanted to be seen with him. Noah shuddered at the thought. Besides, he wanted them around in case Charlie came home to visit.

His mother, Nina, and sister, Shannon, took turns watching the girls this past week but they were busy today and he had a meeting with a new client this afternoon. His brothers, Liam and Simon, were working.

He just needed an hour, so he'd brought Dakota and Dylan to work with him and they'd settled into the chairs in his outer office near his admin's desk.

"Janine," he said to his administrative assistant. "I need you to please watch the girls while I meet with Mr. Canon." A potential new client. "They brought their iPads and can read while I'm busy."

"Umm… sure thing, Mr. Powers," she said, treating the twins to a half smile filled with uncertainty.

In her mid-thirties, Janine was an excellent worker and though she might not love the idea of playing babysitter, he'd make it up to her in her yearly bonus.

"Girls, stay in your seats and I'll be out as soon as I can." He eyed them with his sternest face. "And I mean, do not leave these chairs."

"What if we need the bathroom?" Dylan asked, her lashes fluttering over her green eyes too innocently.

He didn't trust her. They'd asked about Fallon every day since he'd found them at the gallery and he'd insisted she was too busy for them to stop by and say hello. He'd also been forced to insist her painting wasn't right for their apartment. But he was beginning to think the wall the girls wanted to hang the artwork on was perfect.

"Then tell Janine you need the restroom and she'll take you." He wanted them within her sight.

He glanced at his admin. "Eyes on them at all times," he said, his voice gruff. She needed to understand the importance of his request.

"Of course," she said, and her gaze went back to the screen on which she was typing.

"Is Mr. Canon in the conference room?"

She glanced up. "Yes. With his partner."

He nodded, looked to the girls who were both reading, said a silent prayer, and strode out of the room and down the hall.

An hour later, and new client papers signed, Noah returned to his office to find the outer room empty. He assumed Janine had taken the girls to the bathroom or maybe the cafeteria.

Once in his office, he settled into his chair and began to give thought to the strategy for John Canon and his partner, who thought their in-house accountant was embezzling from the business.

"Mr. Powers, I'm so sorry!" Janine ran into the room, teetering on her heels. "One minute they were here, then Mr. Baker called," she said of one of Noah's partners. "And I took some notes and when I hung up, I looked up and they were gone! I searched everywhere in the office but—"

"They're gone," he said, cutting her off with his sharp tone. "Didn't I say not to take your eyes off of them?"

She straightened her shoulders. "In all fairness, Mr. Powers, I'm your admin, not a babysitter. And they're stealthy little things."

He bit down on the inside of his cheek, knowing she was right and he had no intention of firing her. "They're children, not things." He ran a hand through his hair and groaned.

He'd be out of here, looking high and low for the girls once more, if he wasn't certain of where he'd find them.

"But you're right, Janine. They're stealthy. I'm sorry I put you in that position. Can you hold down the fort for the rest of the day?" he asked.

"Yes, Mr. Powers." He shook his head and strode to the elevator, knowing his next stop was the gallery.

To see the woman and the place he'd had no intention of visiting ever again.

FALLON STUDIED THE watercolor by a new client, hanging on the free wall space in the gallery. One of the heavy statue pieces blocked the view of the landscape and needed to be moved.

"Clara?" she called out.

"Yes, dear?" Clara Morganville, the gallery owner, asked from her seat behind her antique desk in the back corner of the room.

Clara had owned the gallery for the last twenty years. Because she also owned the property, when the ceramics store went out of business six months ago, she'd approved Fallon's idea of opening the paint and sip studio next door. They'd broken through the gallery so a door led to the other side, and expanded the business.

"I think this pedestal needs to be moved, don't you?" Fallon gestured to the blocked painting.

Clara rose from the desk and walked around, eyeing the art from all angles. "I can get Oliver to do it for us so we don't have to pay for someone to come in and do heavy lifting."

Since Fallon wasn't facing Clara, she wrinkled her nose. "I didn't know Oliver was in town."

Clara's son was in imports and exports. He traveled often and had been gone well over two months. Despite him being a businessman and Clara adoring him, he'd always made Fallon uncomfortable.

"He's back for a while this time and I'm so happy he's showing an interest in my business. You may find him around the gallery more."

"That's wonderful," Fallon murmured. It wasn't.

Oliver was arrogant, condescending, and lazy. She'd be surprised if they got the pedestal moved sometime this year. She didn't want to upset Clara, so she kept her thoughts about her son to herself.

Chimes sounded from next door where Sylvie was hosting a party, so Fallon wasn't needed on the paint and sip side.

"Fallon?" Sylvie called out seconds later. "You have two little someones here looking for you!" She walked into the gallery with the twins following behind her.

Both girls had big grins on their faces and no parent or guardian with them. When their father realized they were missing, he was going to lose his mind.

"Hi, girls! What are you two doing here… alone?"

They glanced at each other as if each held the answer. "Dad's at work," Dylan said at last.

"And where are you supposed to be?" Fallon asked as she pulled her phone from her skirt pocket, immediately opened it, and tapped the number she'd called him on last time.

Noah answered on the first ring. "Tell me they're with you."

The panic in his voice reached inside her and she looked at his twins. "Yes. I'll keep them with me until you get here."

"Thank you." He breathed out the words in a gruff voice that had her lady parts tingling. She imagined him using that voice while those large hands aroused her and a strangled sound escaped her lips. "See you soon." She quickly disconnected the call.

"Can you tell us about your painting?" Dakota asked.

Fallon sighed. As much as she wanted to lecture them about running off again, it wasn't her place. Noah would burst in soon and handle his children.

Clara walked over, taking her time as she approached from the back end. In her pantsuit and dark hair streaked with gray and pulled into a bun, she appeared the motherly type and acted it as well. She smiled wide when she took in the twins.

"Who do we have here?" she asked.

"Dakota and Dylan, this is Clara Morganville. Clara owns the gallery."

Clara stepped closer. "Hi, girls. I love your names."

"Thanks!" they said at once.

Tipping her head, Clara asked, "Who's who?"

"I'm Dakota." She waved with a grin.

"That must make you Dylan!" Clara applauded herself as if she'd accomplished a miracle.

Both girls giggled, the sound warming Fallon's heart. They were adorable kids.

Though Dylan's hair was down today, as was her sister's, Fallon had figured out the identity question already. She knew Dakota was more likely to give away information and ask questions, while Dylan held back. By personality alone, Fallon could already recognize each twin. By looks? Not so much without a difference in hairstyle and being alerted to identity.

"Look what I happened to find in my bag!" Clara held out two lollipops and the girls grinned.

"What color?" she asked them.

"Red!" Dylan said.

"Yellow." Dakota spoke next.

Clara handed them the candy.

"Thank you," they said, proving Noah and their mother had instilled good manners in them.

Since she didn't know how far Noah's office was from here, she walked the girls over to her painting they'd admired and began to give them a lesson on modern art. Dakota leaned in, soaking in the details while Dylan was more mesmerized by the colors that had drawn her to the painting to begin with.

The chimes above the door jingled and Noah came rushing in, this time in a suit and tie that exuded power. His gaze met hers and heat flared in his eyes. This time she was sure she didn't imagine the mutual awareness between them.

She swallowed hard and waited as he approached. His gaze narrowed as he pinned his girls in place. "Dylan, Dakota, explain. Now."

"We just really wanted to see the pretty paintings again," Dylan said.

"And Janine wasn't paying attention to us at all,"

Dakota added, a whine in her tone.

Who was Janine? Fallon wondered with an unhealthy amount of what had to be jealousy. She didn't like that… at all.

Noah turned an unhealthy shade of red. "Do you have any idea how dangerous New York City is for two girls alone your age?" His voice raised as he spoke. "You could have been kidnapped, for God's sake."

Their eyes opened wide, then shimmered with tears. "We didn't think about that," Dakota said.

"That's right. You didn't think. And apparently neither did I by letting you off lightly last time. Hand over the iPads," he said, hand out.

"But—"

"Now."

They deposited the tablet they'd each clutched against their chest in his open hand.

"And no television for one week."

"Daddy!" they moaned simultaneously.

He shook his head. "No. You'll have plenty of time to think about why these stunts aren't cute. And while you're at it, think about how devastated your mom and I would be if anything happened to either of you."

Though Fallon felt bad for the now crying girls, she understood his anger and the need to follow through with punishment to make his point.

"Stay here while I talk to Fallon," he instructed them.

They huddled together and Fallon followed Noah a few steps away.

Nervous from the situation and wanting to lighten the mood, she said, "You do realize I'll have to start charging for babysitting services if this keeps up?"

Only a slight curve of his lips indicated he found her comment amusing. "I don't know what I'm going to do with them," he said, showing a true hint of vulnerability as he ran his hands through his hair, further messing the strands. "They've run off every nanny to the point where the agency basically fired me. My admin was focused on her computer screen and they disappeared on her to come here."

Janine was his administrative assistant, she realized, hating the relief that washed over her at the knowledge.

Feeling bad for him, she reached out, placing a hand on his shoulder. Even over the suit fabric, she felt the strength in his shoulder muscles.

Ignoring the dangerous sexual awareness she experienced around him, she turned her attention to the issue at hand. "I can understand them missing their mom," she said. "I lost my mother when I was their age."

She skipped the hows of her mother's death. Not

only did she not like to revisit that time, but the idea of someone killing her parent while she was sleeping in another room was still hard to accept or cope with. She'd had enough therapy to function without blaming herself, but it wasn't easy.

His harsh expression softened and she caught a glimpse of the same man he was around his girls. "I'm so sorry," he said.

"Thank you." She swallowed hard. "And I know there needs to be consequences for their actions. I'm just saying… I can understand why they're gravitating to me."

He nodded. "I can, too. Not that I see any real resemblance between you and Charlie. That's their mother. But if they thought so from behind, there will be no changing their minds."

She understood and a sudden thought occurred to her that might help. "Listen, I have an idea. One that would make the twins happy and would give you a break from worrying about them," she said.

He raised an eyebrow. "I'm all ears."

"Right now, our classes at the paint and sip studio next door are for adults. I'm thinking of expanding to giving art lessons to kids but I don't want to turn this into a preschool painting place. Your girls are just the right age and I could have them come in to paint and learn. I could see how they react and if the experiment is something I want to do for real."

He eyed her with an admiring stare. Obviously, she'd said something right.

"I know they'd love the idea, but let's schedule it for after their punishment ends."

"Of course. That's fine." She smiled, excited to teach the twins to paint.

He tipped his head toward the girls and they walked back over to where they stood.

"We're sorry, Daddy," they said in unison, this time, the apology sounding heartfelt instead of rote and Fallon was fascinated how often they spoke the same sentence at the same time.

Noah knelt down so he was at eye level with them. "I love you both so much and I couldn't handle it if something happened to you. Got it?"

"Got it," they chimed together and came in for a group hug.

Watching Noah's affection toward his girls warmed her heart and that was the moment Fallon knew she was in trouble.

"Are we still going out for dinner?" Dakota asked, her tone hesitant.

Noah frowned and Fallon could see he wasn't sure which decision was best.

Finally, he groaned and said, "Considering I didn't plan on cooking, yes. We are."

"Can you come, Fallon?" Dylan asked.

"We're going for burgers and they have world-famous milkshakes. Please?" Dakota put her hands together and pleaded with her to come.

Noah ran his fingers through his hair, a gesture she bet he did a lot where the girls were concerned. Once again, they'd caught him off guard, Fallon thought, trying not to laugh.

He shifted on his feet, obviously uncomfortable and unsure how to get out of the invitation.

"Girls, I'm certain your father wants time alone with you," she said, giving him the opportunity to discuss their wandering tendencies and letting him off the hook.

No need to put him in the position of telling her he didn't want her to join them. The notion already hurt her feelings but she knew having dinner with this little family was a bad idea.

"Please?" Dakota asked. "Don't you like hamburgers and milkshakes?"

She glanced at Noah, beseeching him with her eyes to get her out of this mess.

"Do you like burgers and shakes?" he asked instead, all but inviting her instead of taking the out.

She blinked in surprise. "I do but—"

"Then if you're free for dinner, why don't you join us?"

She didn't know what had changed but she found herself nodding. "I guess I'm coming."

"Yay!" the girls yelled.

Noah stepped closer. "I'm hoping spending time with you will quench their need and not give them a reason to sneak back here. Especially once we tell them about the painting class," he said softly.

In her ear.

In a grumbly, sexy voice that caused her nipples to harden behind her lightweight camisole. His gaze slid from hers to her shirt and she crossed her arms over her chest... too late. His eyes flared before he banked the arousal she'd seen there. That she was still feeling.

Oh, was she in trouble.

Chapter Three

NOAH LED THE girls and Fallon into a 1950s style diner that claimed to have world-famous milkshakes. Black and white checked tiles covered the floor and the seats were a red and white pleather. A huge wall decal of a 1950s red Corvette covered one turquoise wall. Was it over-the-top retro? Yes, but the girls loved it.

The hostess, a middle-aged woman with teased hair to match the decade theme, greeted them with a welcoming smile. "Hello to my double *D*'s!" She greeted the twins with a high five. Glancing at Noah, she winked.

Beside him, Fallon snickered, catching the double entendre.

"Hi, Patty!" they chimed in.

"Your usual booth?" she asked.

Noah nodded. "Thanks."

She glanced at Fallon, curiosity in her gaze since the three came here often and alone. Noah had no intention of explaining. Even he didn't know what the hell he was doing.

Patty led them to a table in the back near the 'Vette

and gestured for them to sit. Dylan and Dakota scrambled into their usual seats, leaving Noah to sit in the cramped booth next to Fallon. Clearly, he hadn't thought this invitation through. The idea was to get her out of the girls' systems, not bring her closer to him.

He gestured for her to slide in. "Unless you want me to?"

She shook her head, gathered her long skirt, and sat down so she could scoot inside. Those crinkled skirts seemed to be a favorite style of hers which led to yet another vision of him hiking up the material, sliding down whatever silky underwear was hidden beneath, and tasting her.

"Noah? Are you going to sit?" Fallon's voice jolted him out of his reverie.

Swallowing back a curse, he slid into the booth and was immediately hit by her sexy perfume, a warm vanilla scent that went straight to his cock. At least now the evidence was covered by the tabletop, he thought, uncomfortable with the entire situation.

"So, girls, what flavor milkshake is the best?" she asked.

"Chocolate!" Dylan exclaimed.

"Strawberry! And Dad likes vanilla." Dakota licked her lips, obviously ready for her shake.

Fallon let out a light, tinkling laugh. "I'm not sure

why I find that amusing, all three of you liking different flavors, but I do."

"What's *your* favorite flavor, Fallon?"

She clasped her hands on the table and leaned forward, utterly engrossed in conversation with his girls. "I'm a vanilla girl, myself," she said.

"Just like you, Dad!" Dylan said.

Noah groaned inwardly, because there was nothing *vanilla* when it came to his thoughts about Fallon.

"What's your mom's favorite?" she asked.

"Strawberry like me." Dakota sounded proud of that fact.

As much as he respected Charlie's need to follow her dreams, Noah hated what her absence did to his kids. They missed her so much sometimes it gutted him.

"Tell me about what your mom is doing in Egypt," Fallon said.

Most women wouldn't think to ask about their mother and he shot her a grateful look. How did Fallon know his girls needed to talk about Charlie and not bury their feelings down deep?

"She's on an archaeological dig," Dakota said, her eyes bright as always when talking about Charlie's work. She was enthralled with learning and unfortunately, the more gruesome parts of the dig, including skeletons.

"She sifts through dirt carefully so they don't ruin the ancient artfacts," Dylan added.

"Artifacts," he corrected, catching the amused lift of Fallon's full lips.

"Can I get you something to drink?" A young, new-to-the-diner, female server walked over to their table.

The girls gave their milkshake order, Noah adding on his and Fallon's.

"Thanks. I'll give you some time to look at the menu and come back," the waitress said and turned to go get their drinks.

"Can we order? I'm starving," Dakota said, drawing out the whine on the last word.

The server paused and shifted her stance, waiting for a decision.

He shook his head. "How about you let Fallon look at the menu first? Just because we come here all the time doesn't mean she knows what she wants to eat."

Fallon placed a hand on his arm, her long fingers curling around his jacket, and damn if he didn't feel as if she'd singed the skin beneath.

"It's fine," she said. "I already know what I want. A hamburger and fries, please."

"See?!" Dakota said.

He groaned and gave their standing orders. The

server departed with their menus.

"So where were we?" Fallon asked.

"Talking about Mom's work. Did you know that after someone died, ancient Egyptians pulled out the brains by sticking special needles up their noses?"

"Eew!" Dylan said.

Dakota shifted so her knees were under her and leaned across the table in excitement. Noah gave her *the look* and she reseated herself in the booth.

"That's… fascinating?" Fallon asked, in search of a suitable adjective and obviously she wasn't sure hers was the right one.

"Dakota, not at the dinner table, okay?" Noah chided his daughter. Nobody needed to eat with the idea of pulling out dead people's brains on their minds.

His daughter folded her arms across her chest and flopped back against the seat with an exaggerated huff. "Fine."

"You can tell me more about the process later," Fallon said.

Noah couldn't help but admire her patience.

The food came out of the kitchen quickly and everyone ate. In between they talked, all discussion of brains forgotten.

He had to remind Dakota not to talk with food in her mouth twice which he considered a positive record.

Dylan pushed for more information about the painting she'd fallen in love with, which led Fallon to ask the girls if they'd like to take a lesson with her. Their excitement for the idea was palpable. Dylan's questions led him to believe he might have a budding artist on his hands, her talent to be determined.

Fallon talked about her dream of owning her own gallery one day and he realized how wrong he'd been about thinking she was flighty in nature. When Dylan asked if all her paintings were in the gallery, she'd shaken her head. She had more at home and two she'd donated to a silent auction for foster children who aged out of the system. Every word she said impressed him more.

"Can we talk about ancient Egyptians and how they mummify dead people now?" Dakota asked.

"No!" He and Dylan spoke at the same time.

"Sure," Fallon said simultaneously.

Leaning back, he stared at Fallon, taking in the slope of her nose, the outline of her plush lips. "You're a trooper," he told her.

Blushing, she shrugged and took a long sip of her milkshake, drawing a big slurp because she'd finished what was in the glass. Just like his kids.

The girls giggled at the sound and he found himself amused.

"How old are you, anyway?" he asked lightly.

"Twenty-five, but you're never too old to drink to the end. Still, excuse me," she said, her cheeks a rosy shade of pink.

Twenty-five. An eleven-year age difference. Jesus fuck. Was that too much? Was she too young for him? And why the hell was he even considering the question?

With full-time custody of his kids and being a partner at the law firm, late at night was the only time that was his and his alone. His freedom for anything or anyone else was severely limited.

And yet Fallon tempted him. Not just her beauty and brains, which he was coming to appreciate, but how she acted around his children. She was quick to smile at them and it wasn't because she was trying to impress him. She showed no jealousy when he focused on the twins. Not that he and Fallon were on a date, but her ability to talk to the girls like they mattered cracked what he thought was his utter disinterest in women for anything other than finding one for occasional relief.

That just left a host of other issues. Their age difference, the fact that he and the twins were a package deal, and his obligations as a parent always came first.

And... whether or not his interest in Fallon was even reciprocated. If it wasn't? Either way, he needed the girls to get chasing after her out of their systems.

Chapter Four

HUMMING TO HERSELF, Fallon stood on a stool, carefully dusting the top of an expensive ceramic piece. Normally, she'd keep her earbuds in but Clara was at the gallery today along with her stuffy, full-of-himself son. Oliver was at the gallery to help his mother set up their newest art exhibit in the room dedicated to showings but she heard him instead regaling Clara about his latest trip abroad.

With his too tight skinny jeans and pompous attitude and arrogance despite his receding hairline, he was hard to put up with. He bragged about his business acumen but since she came from a family of successful businessmen, her gut and the stories of how often Clara had lent him money told her Oliver's claims were false.

But Fallon adored her boss, had even come to think of her as a surrogate mother, so she put up with the man. But it was in her best interest to keep busy so she didn't give him an audience.

"Fallon, would you like a cup of tea? I brought some of the finest leaves home for my mother since she drinks tea often during the day and before bed."

Oliver's voice reached her.

"No, thank you," Fallon said softly, finding it difficult to speak over the sudden lump in her throat at the same time Clara spoke.

"Fallon prefers her caramel lattes." From her seat across the room, Clara treated Fallon to a sympathetic smile, aware of Fallon's painful past.

Tea was a trigger because her late mother loved what she'd called her *teatime*. From the time Fallon was a little girl, she had many tea parties with her mom and as she grew older, the fake pouring turned to sharing the real thing. After her mother was killed, Fallon steered clear of anything reminding her of the bittersweet memories, and once she grew up, she became a coffee drinker instead.

Finished with her careful dusting, she climbed down the ladder, her gaze on the window showcasing the sidewalk and people outside. Stepping onto the floor, she closed the ladder, when she caught sight of a familiar silhouette. The dark hair, shorter on the sides, slightly longer on top, a suit jacket, and handsome profile called to her.

She wondered why Noah was here. And why did her heart skip a beat because he was?

All morning, she'd done her best not to think of dinner with him and the girls last night. She'd had such a good time and enjoyed watching him hide his amusement whenever Dakota said something irreverent or incredibly smart but questionably appropriate.

Noah as a single dad was sexy and she'd be lying if she said she didn't think about him as she'd fallen asleep.

Just as she wondered if he'd come inside, he turned to the window and caught her staring. Feeling the heated blush on her cheeks, she powered through and raised a hand in a wave.

He pulled his hand out of his pants pocket and held it up to her. Without second-guessing, she gestured for him to come inside.

He turned and strode to the door, letting himself in. She gestured for him to wait one second, and walked the ladder to the back before returning to find him staring at *the* painting. Though modern, she'd been more focused on feminine, *bright* colors, so she could see why the piece appealed to the twins. One way or another, she'd be gifting them the art.

"Hi!" She walked up beside him. Sandalwood cologne hit her immediately and the urge to bury her nose in his neck and inhale his sexy scent was strong. Instead, she clasped her hands behind her back and smiled. "So, what brings you by the gallery?"

"I had lunch down the street. I was just on my way back to work."

She nodded. "I thought maybe you were chasing

down the twins again," she said with a grin.

He chuckled but as usual, it wasn't easy to crack his stoic façade. She might just make it her mission to get this man to treat her to a genuine smile.

"I'm curious, Noah. What do you do for fun?" She settled a hand on her hip and cocked her head to the side. "Other than enjoying your girls, I mean."

His sexy mouth turned downward in a frown. "No fair. That was my answer."

"I know. So let's change that. Friday night, there's a band playing at my brother's bar, The Back Door in Tribeca. Meet me there." Making the offer took her off guard. She hadn't meant to say the words but it would be good for him to let loose for one night.

His scowl deepened. "You know I have the girls at home."

"Haven't you ever left them with a sitter for a business dinner? Come on. It'll be fun. Or you can be a grumpy old man and stay home," she said, challenge made.

One she hoped he couldn't refuse because she'd like to see Noah in something other than a suit and tie. She'd been determined not to get involved with another sophisticated, experienced man. And the invitation was dangerous to her resolve. But that hadn't stopped her from taunting Noah into going.

She held her breath and waited for his reply.

"I may be grumpy but I'm not an old man," he

muttered. "I haven't found a sitter yet but I'll ask my sister to watch the girls."

Smiling, Fallon gave him a spontaneous hug, realizing her mistake the moment she felt his hard body against hers, and she stumbled back, putting distance between them. Ignoring her body's reaction wasn't as simple. Between his sexy scent and his muscles that tempted her, her nipples tightened and her sex grew soft and needy, making her happy she wasn't in a lightweight camisole today.

Clearing his throat, he adjusted his tie. "I'll let you know if I can make it," he said, his raspy voice not helping the tingling in her body.

She nodded. "Good. I hope I'll see you there." And she didn't have long to steel herself against his good looks and gruff demeanor that for some reason appealed to her—because it wasn't his roguish charm. He seemed to work overtime not to show her that side of himself. Another thing she was determined to change.

AFTER A LONG day of work, Fallon walked into her apartment, tossed the keys on the kitchen counter along with her purse, and pulled a chilled bottle of pinot from the fridge. After uncorking it, she turned on soft music through her portable speaker and brought the unit into the decent-sized bathroom.

She'd been lucky to find this apartment, renting it from a client of her father's who'd given her a good deal. Considering the Manhattan location, she'd had to dip into the trust fund left to her by her grandparents in order to afford it. Still, she was able to cover a good portion of the rent with her job at the gallery. Her goal was to be self-sufficient but she appreciated the ability to live in a safe area and not need a roommate.

Leaving her wine on the counter, she ran herself a bath, dropping in a bath bomb before she undressed. The days and nights leading up to tonight's gig at The Back Door had been busy. Noah called her the day after he'd walked into the gallery to tell her his sister had agreed to watch the girls, which meant she had a date tonight. Or was it just him responding to her dare? She supposed she'd find out.

But she needed to destress before going out. Between a showing at the gallery on Wednesday night and dinner out with her family last evening, she shouldn't have had time to think about her invitation to Noah but the man was impossible to forget. She couldn't get him out of her mind. In fact, she hadn't had one decent night's sleep without him starring in sex dreams, his large, capable hands arousing her with ease.

With a low groan, she settled into the warm, bubble-filled water, shut the faucet, and leaned back, closing her eyes. The floral smell filled her nostrils and when she picked up her loofah and ran it over her skin, her senses prickled with awareness. It became obvious why the item was labeled, *Sex Bomb: an aphrodisiac jasmine soak for the romantic in you.* She'd have to remember to thank her sister-in-law Raven, Remy's wife, for the gift.

As she unwound, her focus drifted and she wasn't surprised when her thoughts were consumed by Noah Powers. She pushed aside all the negatives that came with getting further involved with a man eleven years her senior, one that reminded her of Ezra and her past. Instead, she decided one night of enjoying the band and dancing with Noah would be okay. Assuming he was even willing to let go and chill.

He was a rigid man, one she sensed didn't bend on his decisions often. She wasn't sure what had pushed her to invite him but she sensed there was an untamed man beneath his outer reserve. As she imagined herself pressed up against his hard body, she slid the loofah over her neck and chest, traveling downward to her breasts. Her nipples puckered at the light raspy sensation and she felt the arousing pull between her thighs.

She let the sponge float in the water, gliding her fingers down her belly and over her sex. Settling her index finger on her clit, she stroked the tiny bud, enjoying the sensations she created in her body. Pleasure suffused her and she raised her hips, her legs stiffening beneath the water.

Lost in the moment, she let her fingers slip lower until she slid one inside, pumping in and out and squeezing her inner walls tight. Pretending it was Noah, she inserted another finger, knowing his would be thicker and longer than her own. On the next press inward, she curled her fingers, rubbing against her G-spot and feeling the rush of enjoyment wash over her.

She moaned and bent her knees. Fingers inside, she rubbed the base of her hand against her sex, the combined sensations taking her higher. The water splashed as she increased her pace. Soon she was soaring, passion washing over her in sensual waves with Noah's name on her lips.

She opened her eyes to find the water tepid and her cheeks burning as if she wasn't alone and had been caught masturbating to thoughts of a man utterly out of her reach. One she sensed could devastate her if she let him in.

A chill took hold and she realized she still sat in the tub, shivering. As she climbed out, she resolved to forget about the past, enjoy her evening with Noah, and not let things get further than that with the smart, aloof, older-than-her attorney. It wouldn't be easy considering she'd just come with his name on her lips.

Chapter Five

NOAH HAD QUESTIONED his sanity every day since he'd let Fallon know he'd meet her at The Back Door tonight. The last time he'd seen her at the gallery had been all his doing. He'd been working until his stomach rumbled, insisting it was lunchtime. He told himself he had a craving for a roast beef sandwich at the deli, which just happened to be around the corner from Fallon's gallery. He also knew he was full of shit.

He'd just wanted to get a glimpse of the woman in flowing skirts and delicate ballet flats with the ever-present smile. None of which explained why he was now walking into the crowded restaurant and bar owned by Fallon's brother, to see a band he had no interest in and the female he couldn't get out of his head. He tried to pay a cover fee at the door, only to be asked his name and told he'd been comped. He'd have to remember to thank Fallon later.

Once inside, he scanned the crowded room, look-ing for her. The spots near the stage and at the bar were the busiest and it was hard to pick anyone out until his gaze landed on a group of people near a hallway. Fallon's profile and shiny brown hair caught his attention and he began to walk toward her, stopping when she threw her arms around a tall, dark-haired man, remaining in his embrace. When she stepped back, he kept one arm around her shoulders as they talked with the rest of the group.

Jealousy sliced through him, taking him off guard, and he strode toward them, determined to remind Fallon *she'd* invited *him* this evening.

As if sensing his presence, she turned and met his gaze, her expressive eyes filled with pleasure.

"Noah! You made it!" She rushed over, grasped his hand, and pulled him into the cluster of men. "Aiden, Jared, Dex, and Remy," she said, pointing to each. "This is Noah Powers, the dad of the adorable twins I told you about. Noah, meet my brothers."

Jesus, he thought, noticing all four men glaring at him. What the hell had he done to deserve that kind of greeting? Then again, that's how he'd treat any guy he didn't know that his sister—or sometime in the very distant future, his girls—brought home.

He extended his hand, unsure whose he'd shake first. Remy, who she'd introduced last, gripped his hand first, squeezing in a definite warning before releasing him. The others followed suit.

By the time they finished, Fallon was shaking her head, her gaze narrowed on her siblings. "You're a bunch of overprotective assholes," she said to them.

Noah reached out and put a comforting hand against her back. "They're just doing their jobs as your brothers."

"And what job is that?" a pretty light brown-haired woman asked, slipping under Remy's shoulder so he was holding her against him.

"I invited Noah to come see the band and Remy is giving him a hard time. You know, that deliberately hard male handshake? They pulled that stunt," Fallon said, her lips twisted in disgust.

The woman stepped back, placing her hands on her hips. "Remy Sterling, leave your sister alone," she ordered, before turning her attention to Noah and looking him over. "Hello, Noah. I'm this Neander-thal's wife, Raven." She smiled warmly at him, her welcome greeting reaching her eyes.

"A pleasure to meet you. And everything is fine here," Noah said.

The other brothers chuckled and both women shot them annoyed glares.

"Come on, Noah. Let's get away from them for a while."

He nodded. "Sure. I'd like a drink. Does anyone want anything?" he asked, being pleasant in the face of their silence.

"No, thank you," came the replies.

She slipped her hand into his, surprising him, and steered him away from her family. Instead of the bar, she led him into the nearby hallway that wasn't as crowded as the main room. "I am so sorry," she said. "I didn't think they'd be such jerks."

"I don't mind them sizing me up. I just don't like that they upset you." And despite him empathizing with their older brother roles, he thought of another reason they were wary. "I'm sure they aren't thrilled I'm a good ten years older than you."

She sighed. "I'm impressed you figured that out. I should tell you, your age is exactly what's bothering them." She nibbled on her bottom lip and he saw the indecision on whether to continue in her antsy body movements as she shifted from foot to foot.

He sensed she needed a push and selfishly, he wanted to learn more about her. "I'm a good listener," he offered.

And they'd eased their way to the nearest wall and he stepped close to Fallon so she didn't have to yell over the din from the outer room.

"The story is a little embarrassing, but here goes. When I was in college, I studied art history." She nibbled some more on her lip and the desire to rub his finger over the spot grew stronger. "Anyway, sophomore year, one of my professors seemed to single me out for his undivided attention. He was cultured and brilliant, and when he spoke to me, it felt like no one else was in the room." She blew out a long breath after the rush of words, rubbing her hands together nervously as she spoke. "Even his name was elegant. Dr. Ezra Manheim encouraged me to come to his office hours and he'd always get to me last, so I was the only one left and we could be alone."

Shit. Noah could see where this was going and he didn't like it one bit. "He seduced you," he said, certain of the outcome.

"It wasn't that difficult." She dipped her head, as if the admission embarrassed her.

It was obvious she blamed herself when in reality, an older man had abused his power and taken advantage of a young woman, he thought with disgust.

"The affair was forbidden. If anyone found out he could lose his job, but he said it was worth it. *I* was worth it. It was intense and I guess because I was young and looked up to him as being so worldly, I thought I was in love. I believed we had a future because he spoke in those terms and lured me in with all the amazing travels we'd do together."

Noah would like to throttle the man. "I'm sorry, sweetheart. He had no right to toy with your emotions." He knew this story wasn't easy for her to tell but he was curious. "What happened?" he asked, keeping his voice gentle.

"Well, the end of my sophomore year, I stopped by his office to surprise him and I found him with an older woman I'd never seen before. She was *his fiancée* who often traveled for work."

He winced on her behalf. "Ouch."

Nodding, Fallon continued. "She had a huge ring on her finger she flashed around as she spoke. After Ezra introduced us, ignoring who I'd been to him, he suggested she meet him at home so he could see what *his student* needed." Fallon shook her head in disbelief.

It was clear she still felt that raw hurt all these years later.

"She left and he informed me our affair was over, since the fiancée I didn't know about had returned. I admit I got hysterical as I asked about all the plans we'd made. He just laughed and called me naïve." She raised one shoulder and dropped it again. "Turns out he picks one female student a year to lavish his affections on and he chose me." Her lips turned downward in a frown he'd never seen on her pretty face before.

"He's a selfish bastard," Noah muttered, just now realizing his hands were clenched in tight fists.

Releasing them, he drew a deep breath and focused on Fallon. He tipped her chin up so she looked him in the eye, her eyes shimmering with unshed tears. "It was a difficult lesson to learn but you survived the rejection and you're better for it. He never deserved you."

"Damn right he didn't." She smiled but it wasn't bright and happy, not that he blamed her.

Just then, a drumroll sounded.

"Oh! The band is starting soon. Come on!" Obviously happy for the distraction, she pulled him out of the hallway, eager to put the memory behind her.

She released his hand and he followed her swaying hips toward the band. But her description of her past relationship left Noah with a sick feeling in the pit of his stomach. He desired her beyond all reason, but he didn't want to be another older man who hurt her in the end.

RELIEVED FOR THE distraction from the soul-baring she'd just done, Fallon started toward the stage. She walked past Brooke, who called her over. She stepped toward her friend with Noah at her back.

"Is everything okay? You were gone a long time," she said, looking from Fallon to Noah who remained silent.

"Of course. We were just... talking." But Brooke knew Fallon as well as she knew herself and she'd obviously read something in Fallon's expression that had her concerned.

She narrowed her gaze. "If you say so, but I'm here if you need me. Here." She held out a full drink. "I haven't taken a sip yet and I can get another one."

"You're a good friend, Brookie," she said, using her childhood nickname. She accepted the glass and took a long sip. "I'm going to get closer to the band. Want to come?"

Brooke shook her head. "I think I'll wait here." Her gaze drifted to Aiden and not for the first time, Fallon wondered what had happened between her sibling and Brooke to make her friend sad when Aiden's name came up or he was around.

"Okay, well, you know where to find me."

Fallon turned to Noah. "Sorry about that. Let's go up front." Once there, she began to sway to the music, the alcohol sliding through her veins and leaving her with a happy, bubbly feeling.

She'd promised Noah fun and she wanted him to let loose and relax for a change. Unfortunately, he remained stiff and unyielding as the crowd filled in around her. Soon she was dancing with other women, moving to the music and enjoying herself, keeping an eye on the sexy man the whole time.

If she couldn't get Noah to dance, she could at least tease him while she did. She loved the feel of the soft gauzy material of her skirt flowing around her legs. And she admitted to herself, she'd chosen her bright-colored cropped top with Noah in mind, knowing she'd bare more of her stomach as she moved.

Noah stood off to the side, his gaze hot as he watched her. Closing her eyes, she raised her arms, undulating back and forth, getting lost in the rhythm of the talented band. If her shirt raised higher as she stretched, even better.

Suddenly, strong arms came up behind her, wrapped around her waist, and pulled her against him, grinding against her rear. Until that unwanted movement, she'd thought Noah had changed his mind but she knew instantly the uptight man wasn't the type to grind in public.

She tried to wriggle out of the man's grasp but he didn't release her. "Let go!" she yelled over the music.

When he refused to listen, she raised her leg and brought her foot down hard on his. Unfortunately, her ballet slipper didn't offer much in the way of weight or pain.

"Bitch!" he yelled in her ear.

Her stomach pitched and suddenly she was free. She spun in time to see Noah grab the man's wrist in his hand. "Ever hear no means no?" A red flush of anger stained his cheeks.

"Let go, asshole," the obviously drunk man slurred.

"Oh, that's ironic," Fallon said.

"I've got this," Remy said, stepping in between her and the jerk of a man. "My bar, my problem."

"My pleasure." Noah released the jerk and he stumbled into Remy, who grabbed the back of his shirt. "Let's go. You're banned." He jerked the man toward the back of the bar where the entrance was located, hence the establishment's name. He looked back at Noah. "Take care of my sister," he said and dragged the complaining guy out of sight.

She glanced at Noah and this time, he grasped her hand and pulled her off the dance floor. "There's a reason I don't come to bars anymore," he muttered, leading her the way her brother had gone.

"Where are we going?" she asked, rushing to keep up with him.

"Outside where it's quiet!" Holding her hand, he strode past the bouncer at the door, a man she knew and waved to, and they burst into the fresh, *quiet*, night air.

Remy, just returning, shot Noah a warning look, and headed inside. She hoped Noah ignored her brother's narrowed gaze. Lord knew she intended to.

"Whew!" she said, catching her breath. "The Back Door doesn't usually get such handsy men. Then again, the band is a new thing and I guess it can lend to a more drunken crowd."

A glance at Noah told her he was still furious. "He put his hands on you," he said, his voice a low growl.

His protectiveness wasn't new to her. She had four brothers, after all. But Noah's kind held more than a hint of possessiveness that she couldn't deny made her want him even more. There weren't many people on the sidewalk. Most were inside where the entertainment was. She took his hand and walked a few steps, luring him into an alcove with more privacy for what she had in mind.

Feeling brave, no doubt due to the alcohol, she slid a hand around his neck, pulled him close, and sealed her lips over his.

Chapter Six

FALLON'S BOLD MOVE startled Noah and he froze for a brief second before reacting, instinct causing him to take over. A low growl escaped his throat as he braced his hands on either side of her face and his tongue teased her lips, pushing past the closed barrier.

Their mouths were fused, tongues tangling, as he tasted the slightly tart yet sweet cranberry juice on her breath. Once her lips parted, she gave willingly, the kiss turning hot and heavy in an instant. Kissing her felt right and when she moaned, rubbing her breasts against his chest despite the fabric between them, he wanted to give her more.

Alone in the alley, he moved one hand to her skirt and began to bunch it up until he reached the hem, enabling him to slide his hand beneath. He slid a hand over her sex, finding her soaking wet for him.

"Jesus, sweetheart." She was so wet he could feel it through her underwear. He slid his thumb over her clit and she jerked her hips toward his finger. "Do you like that? Does it make you wetter?" he asked, pressing in.

"Harder, Noah," she said, curling her fingers into

the material covering his shoulders, pinching his skin.

He dipped his hand beneath the waistband of her barely-there panties, finding a small patch of hair, and when he inched lower, her wet pussy. Meanwhile, his cock was hard and aching against the rough denim, his boxer briefs not providing enough of a barrier.

He'd lost his mind, he thought, pinching her clit, then soothing her with small circles before repeating the action. There was a club of people nearby including her brothers inside and he had his hand up her skirt while she writhed against him, seeking relief.

Something about Fallon made him lose control and whatever common sense he possessed because instead of stopping, he picked up his pace, his movements harder. She liked the small bite of pain he doled out, arching her hips after each pinch, and whispering *harder* in his ear.

He flicked the tiny bud with his thumb and forefinger, then slid one digit inside her wet heat. "I need to come," she said on a whimper, her sex squeezing his finger, his dick throbbing harder. He pumped into her, thrusting in and out, rubbing against her sensitive inner wall.

Her panting became frantic and soon she began to come, her pussy fluttering around his finger, and she cried out, forcing him to place a hand over her mouth so she didn't draw attention to them.

He mentally shook his head at the foolishness of his behavior, all the while, softening his movements and letting her come down from the high she'd just found. He removed his hand from her body, then her panties, adjusting them as best he could.

"I've got it," she said, her cheeks flushed with desire.

They each pulled themselves together in silence, her fixing her skirt, his conscience berating him while his dick was still rock hard. He knew what he'd be doing as soon as he got home tonight, he thought, figuring the shower was his safest bet to find relief. The girls never walked in on him there.

The girls. Fuck. The thought reminded him of who he was and what was important.

"Noah." Fallon's husky voice stopped him from beating himself up more.

He studied her, her lips puffy, her cheeks also red from his move to keep her quiet. He hoped she didn't have the regrets he had. His being that he'd finger fucked her outside knowing someone could walk by and see. Not that he'd kissed her back and made her come. He couldn't bring himself to regret either of those things.

"Are you okay?" he asked in response.

She nodded, a small smile tugging her lips upward. "I'm so good. Come home with me so I can reciprocate," she said softly.

He was shaking his head before he even thought things through. He'd taken advantage of her enough tonight. She was tipsy and he was coming off learning about her painful past with a man close to his age. He'd taken things far enough tonight.

He needed to decide what he wanted from her before he took things any further because she deserved a lot more than a man who would break her heart again.

"Let me take you home. You've had more than a couple of drinks. If this happens between us, it's going to be when you're completely sober."

He felt like shit when she ducked her head and said, "I came with Brooke. We'll go home together." Her cheeks were red, this time from embarrassment, and he kicked his ass the whole way back into the bar.

But there was nothing he could have done to change his answer tonight.

NOAH JUST HAD to be a gentleman, Fallon thought the next morning, as the real mortification of what she'd done set in. She'd thrown herself at the man. *After* he'd made her come against the wall in the alley because she'd kissed him first.

"I am never drinking again," she muttered.

"I agree. I have a splitting headache," Brooke, who'd slept over, said, padding her way into the kitchen looking as shitty as Fallon felt. She picked up a coffee pod and popped it into the machine, making herself a cup of coffee.

Fallon took a sip of her own, savoring the flavor and waiting for a jolt of caffeine.

"You were pretty quiet last night in the Uber home. Want to tell me what had you so off?"

"I made out with Noah. I know that sounds like a teenage thing to say but looking back, that's how it felt. I kissed him first and next thing I knew, we were in the alley and... well, you can imagine."

Brooke's eyes opened wide. "Fallon Sterling, you dirty girl," her friend said, laughing. "Go you. So what happened?"

"I asked him to go home with me and he turned me down." Even now she felt the heat of embarrassment over his rejection rise to her cheeks. "He said I was tipsy and he wouldn't take advantage."

Brooke treated her to a smile, her lips turning upward, as she nodded, obviously impressed. "A chivalrous guy in this day and age. Color me impressed."

"Or turned off by my forwardness. And he's not a guy, he's a man. An older man and if you remember, I've sworn off having anything to do with those."

Brooke sighed. "No two men are alike. You know this."

She wasn't ready to think about the truth in her friend's statement. Instead, she looked at her Apple Watch. "Okay. Saturday's a busy day at the gallery, so I need to get moving."

Brooke waved a hand. "Fine. Try and ignore my wise words but I'll be right here to remind you." She placed her coffee mug in the sink, rinsed, and put it in the dishwasher.

Fallon did the same. "What are you up to today?"

"I need to go home and do laundry," Brooke said with a roll of her eyes. "Everyone's least favorite chore."

Once they were ready, they parted ways, Brooke taking a car home to the gatehouse where she lived with her mom while she saved money, and Fallon took the subway to work. Unlike Jared who preferred a driver, she and Aiden preferred the subway. It was faster than sitting in traffic.

A little while later, she arrived at the gallery, stopping at the café on the corner to buy a breakfast treat. She walked through the door, a bag with a scone inside in one hand, to find Clara had arrived early. She sat in the back behind her desk, Oliver peering over her shoulder. No doubt she had the gallery financials pulled up on the computer because that was the only thing he was interested in when it came to the business. The accounting, not the art.

"Good morning," Fallon said, keeping her voice cheery despite Oliver's unwanted—at least by her—presence.

"Hello, Fallon," he muttered, straightening from his position by the computer.

"Good morning," Clara said, in a dull voice.

One look at Clara and Fallon knew something was wrong. Her face was pale and her lips were pursed tight. "Is everything okay?"

"Mother was just telling me she wasn't feeling well. She's nauseous and dizzy," Oliver said.

Fallon immediately walked over to her friend and sat down across from her antique desk. "I think you should make a doctor's appointment with your cardiologist," she murmured. "Maybe it's something related to your heart condition." Reaching out, she covered Clara's more weathered hand with her own.

"Or maybe it's a virus and she just needs to go home and rest," her son said.

Fallon narrowed her gaze. At his mother's age, it was careless to make assumptions about what was wrong with Clara. "Clara, can I at least take you home?" she asked. Although she hated to leave Oliver here alone, he could handle business until she returned.

"That might be best," Clara said. "I'm quite dizzy."

"I'll take you." Oliver spoke in a tone that didn't allow for an argument, especially when he grasped his mother's elbow and helped her from the chair. "Let me get you settled in bed. I'll make your favorite tea," he said, then glanced at Fallon. "Mother loves the tea I brought back from abroad. Are you sure you don't want to try some? The spiced chai is delicious."

"No," she said, more firmly than she had the last time he'd offered. Maybe he'd stop trying to push his tea on her.

He readied his mother to leave, making sure she had her purse, and waited for Fallon and Clara to coordinate opening tomorrow if Clara needed to stay home. He tapped his foot in a steady beat, his impatience showing.

"Sylvie will be here soon to help cover the floor. Don't worry about a thing. I can run this place for as long as you need."

Clara smiled. "I know you can. You're indispensable to me."

Her throat filled with emotion. Clara and her kindness often collided with memories of her mother. They were both lovely, refined, and so sweet.

"Go home and rest," she said, studying Clara, concerned about her pallor. "I'll call you later and see how you're feeling."

Oliver visibly gritted his teeth. "She has me. She'll be fine," he bit out.

Was it jealousy over their relationship? Fallon shrugged and decided not to waste any more time thinking about Oliver and his eccentricities. The last thing she wanted was to upset an already ill Clara.

Oliver and his mother departed, leaving Fallon alone at the gallery. The weather was gorgeous and the day passed quickly, a ton of browsers coming in and out. She sold one of her favorite pieces to a man who needed an anniversary gift for his wife, promising to deliver while she was at work next week.

When she finished, Fallon walked into the painting side where Sylvie was setting up the easels for tonight's group of women. They'd booked the evening to celebrate someone's thirtieth birthday, and those type of evenings usually meant a lively group. Although she usually enjoyed overseeing them, she was glad Sylvie was managing the night alone.

She and Sylvie talked for a bit, then Fallon left her alone to finish readying the room. Back at Clara's desk, she picked up her bag which she'd stored beneath the desk after the other woman left, accidentally moving the mouse. The computer came to life. Sure enough there was a P&L statement on the screen. With a sigh aimed at Oliver, who'd probably been asking his mother for money, she shut down the machine for the night.

She glanced at her watch and saw it was almost five. Time to head home where she planned to pour herself a glass of pinot, take a warm bath, and not masturbate to thoughts of Noah.

The chime of her cell phone was a welcome interruption and she hoped it was one of her siblings so she could make dinner plans during the week. A distraction was exactly what she needed to take her mind off of the man who'd turned her down, even if it had been the right thing to do. She'd been tipsy enough to suffer a hangover the next morning, so she was glad he'd respected her enough to say no. Even if it hurt her feelings.

Retrieving her phone from inside her bag, she was shocked to see Noah's name on the screen. After two run-ins with the girls, she'd saved his number and her stomach fluttered at the sight.

She swiped to answer the call. "Hello?"

"It's her!" she heard a familiar girl's voice say.

"Say hello!" her sister said.

"Dylan or Dakota?" she asked, laughing.

"Dakota, and I don't have a lot of time. I borrowed Daddy's phone."

Why was she not surprised, she thought and shook her head in amusement. "Hi, honey. What's going on?"

"Daddy might come back any minute and he can't know we're calling. So, when can we come paint like you promised?"

No point in telling the girls their father would see her number in the list of calls and realize what was going on. They'd find out soon enough.

"I think that's up to your dad." He'd have to call her and set up a time.

Dakota groaned. "He's been busy makin' nanny appointments with people we are *not* going to like."

"We really won't!" Dylan chimed in. "But Aunt Shannon has the flu and Grandma said she can't watch us every day. Just the days she doesn't have cansta."

Cansta? Fallon was going to have to figure that one out later.

"You haven't even met the person yet. How do you know you won't like them?" she asked.

"We just *know*…" the young girl said, drawing out the word.

"Dakota Powers, who are you on my phone with?" Noah's angry voice sounded.

"Uh-oh, gotta go!"

Fallon expected her to disconnect the call but instead she heard Noah's deep, sexy voice. "Hello?" he asked more than stated.

She gripped the phone harder. "Hi, Noah. It's Fallon."

"Girls!" he bellowed at them. "Go to your room and we'll discuss you sneaking my phone off my dresser later."

"Hey, Fallon."

"Hi." The word came out mid-laughter. "I'm sorry. I can't help it. They're just so… so… precocious," she said.

"That's one word for it. I'm sorry they bothered you."

She envisioned him running a hand through his hair, tousling the soft strands in frustration. "They're no bother. Honestly. I enjoy them." Probably more than she should considering she was attracted to their father.

He cleared his throat. "I meant to stop by today to talk. About Friday night. But my sister had the flu and couldn't watch the girls and Mom had her weekly canasta game."

"Canasta," she said, the word now making sense. "So that's what cansta means." She let out another laugh.

"Yes." Even he chuckled. "What did they want?" he asked of his daughters.

"To plan a time when they can come paint. They said you're busy scheduling nanny appointments, and I quote, with people they're not going to like." She paced around the back area of the gallery as she spoke.

Another groan left his throat. "I do not know what I'm going to do with them. My family is helping when they can but my brothers work and you know the rest. Speaking of work, I need to get back to it. At least my mother has them tomorrow."

She felt for him. She really did. "Well, why don't we plan something they can look forward to? That might ease the pressure a little if they're excited about something. I can work with them tomorrow night. We aren't booked for a party and we aren't open Tuesday evenings for painting, so no one will come in at the last minute." Painting wasn't something they did every night of the week.

"I hate to reward them but truthfully, that would be perfect. If I can't leave the office by five, my sister can take them for dinner—assuming she's better—and come by the gallery after, if that works for you?"

"It does." And Fallon was looking forward to spending time with the twins.

"Thanks. Now I have to go discipline two naughty nine-year-olds."

"Good luck," she said with a smile on her face.

"Fallon?"

Her heart skipped a beat. "Yes?"

"We *will* have that talk."

She'd blocked out his mention of that comment in the beginning of the conversation and there wasn't much she could say now. She had a hunch when Noah wanted something, he knew how to get it.

She wondered if that included her.

Chapter Seven

THE NEXT NIGHT, after a long day of running the gallery alone because it was Sylvie's day off, Clara stayed home again, and Fallon prepared for the twins' visit. When the door opened and two little tornados of energy came in giggling and chattering, she smiled. Behind them was a pretty woman who strongly resembled her brother, especially in her green eyes, so much like the girls.

"Hi. I take it you're Fallon?"

She nodded.

"Shannon Powers." She greeted Fallon with a warm smile. "I'm happy to meet you. The girls haven't stopped talking about you. I admit to being curious."

"This is the painting we love, Aunt Sha!"

Shannon smiled. "I've heard a lot about that too." She gazed lovingly at her nieces, her lips lifting as she looked at them. "It's gorgeous, girls." She refocused on Fallon. "You're very talented."

"Thank you," Fallon murmured.

"Have they worn Noah down yet?" Shannon asked.

"Actually," she said to Shannon. "I think he's torn

between not rewarding their behavior and giving them what they so desperately want. I admit, I'm sure it's the bold colors that attract them to it." And she couldn't help but be amused by their persistence, probably because she wasn't a parent nor was she the one who had to make a choice.

Shannon narrowed her gaze as she studied her. Not in an angry way but a perceptive, thinking one. "I believe it's more than that. You remind them of Charlie in some ways. And you treat them with respect. They like you. A lot. And if you don't mind my saying so, I think my brother does too."

On that note, Shannon turned to the girls. "Ready to paint?"

Oh, she was a slick one, Fallon thought, and she liked her even if Shannon's words made her nervous. A sober Fallon hadn't yet figured out what she wanted from Noah.

She'd chosen a unicorn with a multi-colored mane for the girls to paint and the session went extremely well. Dakota asked detailed questions about the project while Dylan lost herself in the creative aspect. One of the reasons she'd wanted to open up one night for preteens was to offer a creative outlook and expression. Painting reached all different personalities for different reasons. As the girls worked, Fallon and Shannon bonded over a book they were both reading, and the time passed quickly.

They were just finishing up when Noah arrived, looking harried and rushed as he entered the front door of the painting studio.

He'd loosened his tie, had his jacket over one arm, and once again the shirt sleeves were rolled, showing those sexy forearms. She'd never thought of forearms as sexy before and wondered why she kept noticing it on Noah. She supposed for the same reason when she inhaled, his cologne took her back to Friday night. Everything about the man attracted her.

"Hi, everyone," he said, his gaze lingering on Fallon before focusing on the twins. "I tried to get out earlier. Girls, how's it going?"

"Daddy, look!" They each pointed at their easels and he strode over, giving them his full attention. Damned if she didn't find that sexy as well.

He was a good father. Solid, like hers was, she thought, and found herself smiling.

"Beautiful! Really great job!" The approval in his tone lifted that normally gruff voice. Glancing at Fallon, he gave her a small incline of his head. A thank-you. His approval warmed something deep inside.

Shannon leaned in close. "I think someone likes my brother, too," she whispered, and before Fallon could answer, she picked up her purse. "Noah, I can take the girls for ice cream and meet you at home. Dakota, Dylan, who wants a treat?" Her words and excited tone preempted Noah from objecting and he narrowed his gaze.

Shannon ignored him. She merely hustled the girls to clean up and get their things.

"I'll be home shortly," Noah said, frowning at his sister. "I should make you stay over. They'll never fall asleep with all that sugar."

Shannon smirked at him, patting him on the cheek. "You can thank me later," she whispered.

He rolled his eyes and walked her and the girls to the door. "Be good," he warned them.

"We're always good, Daddy," Dylan said innocently.

"We are. Do you want ice cream?" Dakota asked.

Noah managed a smile. If only he could lie to himself the same way as his precocious girls.

He shook his head because he didn't want ice cream. He did, however, hope he'd get a taste of Fallon as his sweet treat. "No thanks. Go. Have fun."

Shannon waved and they walked out the door.

Noah breathed a sigh of relief, then turned, his focus on Fallon. "So."

She tucked a strand of hair behind her ear and he realized she had a streak of white paint on her cheek. He strode over and keeping his gaze on hers, lifted a hand and rubbed her soft skin with his thumb. "Paint," he said, chuckling.

"I like that sound."

He raised an eyebrow. "What sound?"

"You laughing. You don't do it nearly often enough."

He didn't? "I laugh with the girls." He made sure they received all his love and affection. As much as he could give. "As for the rest, life is serious, don't you think?"

"Sometimes. But sometimes you need to look through a different lens and let yourself enjoy it. Like the night at the bar…" Her voice trailed off and a blush filled her cheeks, the obvious memory of their time in the alley fresh in her mind. And his.

He'd gone to sleep with thoughts of her in his head, dreamed of taking that kiss further, of more than his hand between her slick folds. His cock tented his slacks and he had no doubt if she looked down, she'd notice.

"About that night, I wanted to make one thing clear."

She looked up at him with wide, golden brown eyes, her lips slightly parted, and he swallowed hard before continuing.

"I didn't turn you down because I don't want you. I just wanted you clear-headed. And now that I've had time to think, I realize how complicated this could be. I have the girls to consider and they've grown attached to you already."

She bit down on her lower lip and he released it from captivity with one finger, rubbing over the redness there.

"I've been thinking too, and I really should thank you for being a gentleman. Though not too much of a gentleman," she mused.

"The alleyway," he said, reading into what she hadn't spelled out.

She ducked her head, a shy smile on her face. Another thing he appreciated about her, her openness and honesty. No airs or fakeness about her. "I should tell you up-front, I'm not looking for a serious relationship. I know what happened with Ezra was a few years ago and I'm over him, but the damage is still there. The ability to hand over my heart easily... I lost that, thanks to him."

Once again, Noah wanted to find the man who'd used her so carelessly and teach him a lesson. Instead, he could show her that it was okay to trust again by being honest in return.

"I admire your honesty as much as the fact that you know yourself so well."

She lifted one shoulder. "My mother said I was an old soul back when I was ten." Her eyes misted and it struck him deeply how much she missed her parent.

It gave him some insight into what his girls might be feeling with Charlie so far away, and the fresh understanding would go a long way toward helping him talk to them when they acted out. As for Fallon, his heart broke for her, and knowing she'd been almost the same age as the twins are now gave him equal appreciation for how difficult it must have been for her to lose her mother.

"Hey. Want to go grab something to eat? I came straight from the office and I'm starving."

A soft smile lifted her lips. "Buy me a slice of pizza?"

"I didn't know you'd be a cheap date." He shook his head, learning to expect the unexpected from her.

She grabbed a leather jacket from a hook in the back and began shutting off the overhead lights, leaving just the sconces illuminating the paintings on the walls. A glance at the closed door leading to the gallery told him that side had already been locked up.

He escorted her out and she took him to her favorite pizza place nearby where she introduced him to the owner, an older Italian gentleman who obviously had a soft spot for Fallon. They shared a small pizza and talked about everyday things. The twins, their antics, how they did in school, and how Fallon fit personal painting into her busy work schedule.

She talked to him about her looking at her boss as a mother figure and how she worried about her son taking advantage of the older woman and even more, she was concerned about her health. Essentially, he got to know Fallon better and vice versa.

After, he walked her to the Uber she insisted on taking and asked her to call or text when she was home, locked up in her apartment, safe.

Noah went home to the twins, only to listen to even more talk about Fallon.

Chapter Eight

NOAH ARRIVED AT the diner to meet with the first woman he'd be interviewing for the nanny job for the duration of the summer. He'd decided to take the time away from work and not the girls to handle the interviews. The woman was already five minutes late, which did nothing to impress him. He wasn't thrilled with the candidates so far, including the women he'd tried in the past. The last straw was the older woman the twins ran away from and they'd already made it clear they didn't plan on liking anyone he brought home this time around.

He leaned back in the chair and his thoughts drifted to the same place they usually did. To Fallon and how perfect she was with his daughters. She knew how to make them laugh, distract them from boredom, tap into what meant a lot to each girl. She'd immediately caught on to the fact that Dakota was tougher with a soft inside she didn't always show, while Dylan was more mushy on the outside but when it came down to it, she knew how to stand her ground, just like her sister. Noah and Charlie understood their unique personalities and it meant something to him that

Fallon did, too.

Since the night they'd shared pizza, he'd been too busy to make a date to see her and he'd been stupid enough not to pin her down at the time. Instead, the few times he'd left the office for lunch, he walked past the gallery, well aware he had no time to stop in, so he'd have to make do with a simple glance—of her profile, her long hair hanging over her shoulder or down her back, or if he was lucky, a quick glimpse of Fallon smiling or laughing at something someone had said.

"Mr. Powers?"

His name snapped him back to the present. To the young woman who wasn't dressed appropriately for an interview. Her T-shirt was pulled tight across her breasts, the lace running between barely covering her exposed cleavage. Tight jeans only added to the fitted look. Her appearance was making it difficult to hold on to hope that she'd be the answer to his prayers and his girls' next nanny.

He rose to his feet. "Annie Jones?"

She nodded and smiled, "Yes, hi!" She lowered herself into the chair across from him before he could pull it out for her.

He settled back into his seat.

"I'm sorry I'm late. I missed my first train."

He nodded and decided to start out with complete

honesty. "As I said to the recruiter who set up this interview, I leave the house at seven-thirty a.m. to be in the office by eight. Is that going to be a problem for you?" Because he chose not to have a live-in nanny when he was with his children in the evenings and early morning.

She shook her head. "Gosh, no. I'd be on time."

"Good. Now, tell me about yourself and why you want to watch children?" He asked the first question from his prepared questions.

She cleared her throat and straightened her shoulders. "I'm good with kids. I used to watch my cousins. And during the year I can go to one of the local colleges."

"And what do you plan to study?"

"Social work."

"Admirable," he said, and continued on with his questions, noting that somehow she seemed to move her chair closer to his as time went on.

"Tell me about your cooking skills? As you know, the girls will need breakfast, lunch, and dinner." Although he planned on trying to be home for the latter meal and spending the evening with them, including making their dinners, he still wanted answers. In case he needed to work late.

She tucked her brown hair behind her ear and leaned in, one elbow on the table, those ample breasts too close for comfort. "I'm a good cook. I can make sure you have everything you need meal-wise, as well as the children. I don't mind taking care of all of *you*." Her emphasis was on the last word and she fluttered her heavily mascaraed eyelashes.

And he was ready to call this one a bust. No pun intended.

"I'm concerned with the girls, not myself, Ms. Jones." His tone left no room for misinterpretation. He wasn't interested in anything she had to offer him.

"That's a pity because I'm so eager to be all things to everyone. Including you. I did my research on you too, Mr. Powers, and that's why I was hoping we could turn this into a live-in position." She slid her hand over his, the unwelcome gesture taking him off guard.

Before he could pull his hand away, he felt the heat of someone's stare. The sense he was being watched. He glanced up to see Fallon had walked into the diner, an older woman by her side. Her gaze dropped to where Annie's hand was on his. He jerked free but the hurt in Fallon's eyes told him the damage had been done. She averted her gaze and escorted her companion to the free table the hostess had shown them.

"I'm sorry, Ms. Jones. This won't work out. Excuse me."

"But—"

He tossed money on the table to compensate the waiter for the time he'd taken and rose to his feet. Fallon sat in a booth across from the elegant woman whose cane rested against the bench.

Steeling himself, he strode over to them. She steadfastly stared straight ahead, ignoring him, though she must know damn well he was there.

"Good afternoon, ladies."

"Hello to you," the woman with Fallon said. "Well, isn't he a sight for these aging eyes?"

"Behave, Clara." Fallon's lips curved into an unwilling smile.

"Clara Morganville," she said, ignoring Fallon and putting out her weathered hand.

He took it and clasped it gently in his. "Noah Powers," he said. "It's a pleasure to meet you in person. I've heard so much about you from Fallon." Who still wouldn't meet his gaze.

"Aah, but I can't say the same. That's something we need to rectify."

He liked her already. "Would it be okay if I borrowed Fallon for a few minutes? I need to speak with her."

"Actually, I need to go powder my nose."

Fallon narrowed her gaze. "Your nose looks fine to me. But if you need to, I want to make sure you're steady. I'll go with you."

"I'm feeling a little better."

Noah took a better look at Clara, taking in her grayish pallor, understanding Fallon's concern for her boss.

"I know I can make it to the restroom in the back. You two talk." Clara pushed her way out of the booth and Noah took her hand again and helped her to her feet, then handed her the cane.

She slowly made her way to the back of the diner, Fallon watching her with a steady gaze until she disappeared from sight. He waited for that moment and slid into Clara's side of the booth.

Fallon had picked up a menu and was studying it in silence.

"Hey. It's not what it looked like. I'm going to go out on a limb and say you know it, too." He tapped the top of the menu until she lowered it, revealing her face. Her beautiful eyes held a hint of sadness, and there was no normal Fallon cheerfulness that he enjoyed.

She swallowed hard. "We aren't in a relationship, Noah. Whatever you do… or don't do isn't my business."

"And yet you walked in here, saw me with a young woman, and were hurt. Sounds like that makes what was happening your business."

"Fine." She placed the menu on the table and met

his gaze. "I was surprised to see you with someone. Eventually I remembered you were having nanny meetings and I was being ridiculous for a number of reasons. One being that we aren't in a relationship so it shouldn't matter to me. I promised myself I wouldn't let you matter." Her eyes shimmered and he cursed to himself.

Ouch, he thought, though he appreciated her honesty. Based on her past, he also wasn't surprised by her feelings. There was a positive side, though. "Apparently, you weren't successful. It seems like I *do* matter. Which makes this the perfect time to tell you that despite my own reservations, I feel the same way."

She nibbled on her bottom lip. "Promise me something, then."

He raised an eyebrow. "Name it."

"Don't ever use the expression, *it's not what it looks like*, again."

Noah immediately understood why and knew it had everything to do with the bastard who'd hurt her. "Done. Now you can do something for me."

She'd curled one hand into a fist, her tension obvious, so he reached out and pulled her fingers away from her palm, taking note of the nail marks left behind with a frown.

"What is it?" she asked.

He slid his fingers into hers, entwining them together. "Don't compare me to your ex. I don't know what this is any more than you do. But…" He slid out of his side of the booth and into hers.

Startled, she let out a little gasp.

He grasped her chin in his hand and leaned in close, the warm vanilla-based scent of her chosen fragrance sending awareness shooting through his veins. "Fallon, I know who I am and who I'm not. And I'm not the kind of guy who plays games." From the corner of his eye, he saw Clara slowly making her way back to the table.

Fallon nodded at his words, her body still upright and uptight but from the slight drooping of her shoulders and the slow breath she exhaled, he sensed he'd gotten through to her.

"Tell me you're not trusting that girl with the twins," Fallon said, wrinkling her nose in disgust.

He let out a harsh laugh. "Hell, no. I need someone to watch the girls, not a woman to seduce me. Besides, I was already seduced last week by the only female I'm interested in."

Her lips parted and Noah leaned in, capturing Fallon's mouth in a brief kiss before letting her go. "Think about that," he said, and slid back, then rose from his seat in time to nod at Clara who'd just approached. He helped the older woman into the booth and steadied her cane against the edge of the table.

"Have a good day, ladies," he said, winking at Fallon before walking out of the diner.

Only when he was on his way home did he realize what he'd done. He'd winked. A gesture he'd never used before with anyone else. A lighthearted one that he felt sure Fallon would appreciate. She'd gotten to him in so many ways in such a short period of time.

He shoved his hands into his slacks pockets and walked back to the office, his mood lighter from seeing Fallon, despite the lack of a nanny and the concerns they obviously both had about one another. For him, it was the age difference, the fact that he'd lived his life with kids and one day, no doubt, she'd want her own. And her wariness was completely understandable.

But nothing would stop him from seeing her. It was as if she called to him, and there was no way he'd put her out of his mind and forget.

AFTER A FULL day's work, Noah arrived home and relieved his mom. The girls were excited that the weekend was coming, reminding him they were going to his parents' on Sunday for his mom's birthday. He didn't know how the visit had slipped his mind but he'd already bought the gift, so at least that was taken care of.

"Are you excited, Daddy? Grandpa said he bought Grammy's favorite cake and you know it's mine too," Dylan said.

"Chocolate." Dakota wrinkled her nose.

"Oh, stop. Strawberry is weird! Besides, Grammy said she'd make you those yucky strawberry jam cookies. Disgusting."

"Strawberry was the first fruit to be used at an ice cream parlor in 1776."

"It's fruit!" Dylan wrinkled her nose this time.

He ran a hand through his hair, grateful they weren't talking about pulling brains through dead people's noses. Still, he wasn't in the mood for their bickering. "Okay, girls. Enough. I've had a long day. Grandma said she left warm lasagna on the counter. Who wants to eat?"

"We helped her cook and set the table!" Dylan ran into the kitchen, Dakota on her heels.

"Girls, who wants to invite a friend over tomorrow?" This way he could get some work done while they played with the school friends they missed. He was lucky he'd found a diligent first-year associate who wanted to work his ass off to one day be partner. He made Noah's life so much easier but no matter how much work he had, he'd always put his girls first. And after that last interview, he was at a loss about hiring someone who could care for them the way they deserved.

"I want Olivia!"

"Jenny!"

Each girl named a friend and asked to make the call to invite them over themselves. After the meal, he handed over his phone while he cleared the table, rinsed, and placed the dishes in the washer.

Plans made, he was about to suggest they take a bath or shower when Dakota spoke. "Dad?"

He lifted his head, always sad when they skipped over daddy for the more adult word. It didn't happen often and he prayed it took a long while for them to grow up further and truly lose their little girl behaviors. "What's up, kiddo?"

She glanced at her sister and he braced himself because that look meant they'd been talking. Which usually meant scheming. "Dylan and me—"

"Dylan and I," he automatically corrected.

"Dylan and I," she parroted, "want to invite Fallon to come with us to Grandma and Grandpa's this weekend."

He shut the dishwasher door and turned to see their overly angelic faces. Wide eyes, earnest looks. He sighed and before he automatically answered no, he decided to give it some thought. "Tell you what. You two go take your showers or baths and I'll let you know when I come tuck you in later. Sound good?"

"Yes, Daddy. We miss her." And on that proclamation, they rushed out of the kitchen, their voices too low for him to hear.

As he sprayed the table and finished cleaning, his thoughts went to Fallon, the girls, and Charlie. They told him they spoke to their mom, showed her the paintings they'd made, and mentioned their mom had a lot of questions about the woman who'd given them the lesson. No doubt because they'd chattered non-stop about Fallon.

Fallon, who gave the twins her time. Who had patience and understanding while their mom was out of the country. He put away the bottle, tossed the rag in the laundry area off the kitchen, and walked into the living room and sat down.

Did he want to take Fallon to his family and deal with all that would signal to his parents and siblings? He glanced out the window to the darkening evening sky, as always, appreciating the glittering lights from other buildings and apartments around the city. Looking outside always helped center him after a crazy day and let him think. And the fact was, he didn't have to think long. His feelings for Fallon were real and growing. He couldn't deny them if he wanted to.

When he'd seen her walk into the diner, his entire

body had responded and not just in a sexual way, though that was a given. Seeing her had lightened his mood—until he'd hurt her feelings—and the warmth in his chest wasn't the typical reaction to a female he was friendly or worked with.

He no longer wanted to push his feelings—or her—away. If he invited her to his folks', it was a casual family dinner. Nothing to send himself or her into a panic.

He and the girls wanted to spend time with her. He could make it that simple. It was that simple, he told himself, aware he was falling harder with every lie he spun.

Pushing himself to his feet, he strode toward the bedrooms to make sure the twins had begun their nightly routine. And to let them know he'd made his decision.

Chapter Nine

FALLON WAS HAVING a crappy day. Her siblings were getting together for lunch at Remy's bar and she'd had to cancel because she was alone at the gallery. Sylvie's cold had lingered and turned into a bad case of the flu and Clara had called her, saying she wasn't feeling up to coming to work today. The art studio had a late afternoon class booked and instead of a slow gallery day, the store was more busy than usual.

With Clara so ill, Fallon was going to have to bring up the idea of hiring another sales associate or someone full time who wanted to teach the classes. All Fallon knew was she'd been running herself ragged.

Lunchtime arrived and she knew there was no way she could take a break. Thank goodness she was able to drink the coffee their machine brewed.

During a free minute, she took a sip and moaned her delight, just as the door opened and a man with a tall ladder strode in. "Great," she muttered, placing her cup down and striding over. "Karl, I expected you this morning," she said to the electrician.

"Sorry. We had an emergency. All hands on deck. What can I do for you and Clara?" he asked. "The boss said something about a flickering light?"

She nodded. "Over that sculpture." She pointed to the metal piece on a podium in the center of the gallery. "Be careful!" she called as he headed in that direction. "Watch out for the customers," she said under her breath and rushed over to where a young couple were attempting to get a better look at their newest item, which was why they'd centered it under that particular light.

"Hi. Can I show you some of this artist's other work? Just until the light is fixed," she explained, drawing them away so Karl could place the ladder.

Thirty minutes later, she was wondering how she'd ever have time to set up the party room for the class when the door opened and a welcome distraction walked inside.

Noah was dressed in his usual shirt and tie but he left his jacket at the office. Instead, his sleeves were rolled, revealing his muscular forearms, and she was glad for the warmer weather today. She didn't have much time but she'd find some for him.

He walked over, his easy stride yet another attractive thing about him. "Fallon, hi."

"Hi! This is a nice surprise."

He glanced around the busy showroom. "But it doesn't seem like a good time."

She sighed. "Clara and Sylvie are both out sick. I'm

worried about my boss. She's usually spry and ready to do anything. Meanwhile, I have a party in an hour that I need to set up for, the electrician was late and is now making a mess in the middle of the showroom, and we're packed with people who seem interested in buying. I'm just one person and—"

He braced his hands on her shoulders. "Breathe."

She listened and drew in some much-needed air, letting it out again.

"Good. Now, what's the priority? And no, you can't say everything." An almost-smile tugged at his lips.

God, she wanted to kiss him again, she mused, then shook her head. "Setting up for the party."

He nodded. "Then go. I'll wrangle things in here."

She raised her eyebrows, certain she was so surprised, they'd hit the roof. "You can't—"

He squeezed one shoulder. "I can."

"You have work!"

He shrugged. "I can take the afternoon off."

"But the girls?" She tried again to find a reason he couldn't possibly stay and help, no matter how much she needed the hand.

"Are with my brother, Liam. I promise you, I can help out."

Her lips parted and he leaned in just as Karl yelled out, "Can someone hang onto the ladder?"

She swung out of Noah's grasp as he clasped one hand in hers and redirected her toward the painting room. "You go set up. I'll get him out of here and do what I can to help some of your customers."

Unable to stop herself, she hugged him tight, inhaling his warm, musky scented cologne. "Thanks, Noah. I owe you one."

He squeezed her waist and said, "Don't worry. I plan to collect."

Thanks to his husky voice and assertive touch, her sex pulsed with need. Not the time, she warned herself, and rushed into the other room, leaving Noah to handle the chaos she left behind.

NOAH HAD A new admiration for Fallon's work. His days were spent behind a desk. Hers were on her feet, and he jumped from potential buyer to potential buyer, only able to help the ones who didn't want a full understanding of the artist behind the sculpture or painting they were interested in.

Still, he sold one, took another's information so Fallon could make an appointment for them to come back another time, and sent a few women into the painting side for their class. At the end of the day, he walked into the classroom side and saw Fallon was wrapping up the class, so he sat down on a chair in the back and groaned in exhaustion.

What did it say about his feelings for Fallon that he'd skipped an entire half day of his own job to help her out? Before he could muse on that question, she strode into the back and joined him.

"You're still here! I wouldn't have blamed you if you locked up the gallery and snuck out while I was busy with the women next door."

Her soft smile and the gratitude in her voice made his entire day worthwhile. That answered his question. He was falling hard for this woman and it was time to step things up. Other than watching out for the twins' feelings, he was finished tiptoeing around his own.

"I said I'd stick around and help."

"And I cannot thank you enough." She dropped into the seat beside him, letting her shoulders slump and the day's exhaustion catch up with her. "But you never did say why you walked in here in the first place."

"Oh, that."

She laughed. "Yes, *that*."

"The girls and I are going to a family birthday party for my mom on Saturday. It's a casual thing at my parents' house and we'd like it if you came along."

Her eyebrows rose high. "Come to your parents'?"

He swallowed a laugh. He'd hoped by using the

twins, he'd soften that point and make it less a date when in his mind, it was every bit one. "Like I said, it's casual and we'd all really like it if you joined us."

She changed from her relaxed pose, sitting up straighter in her chair and leaning toward him, her gaze focused on his. "Noah, is this a date or bring the woman the twins are currently obsessed with to a fun family gathering, no stress?"

He respected her need for honesty and he could give her no less in return. "It's a bit of both." He leaned in closer. "I want to spend time with you. And if you can get past the older guy thing, I want... more." He couldn't say what that meant right now other than being with her and seeing where things between them went.

He'd never brought a woman around the twins and understood the magnitude of doing so. Add in the fact that Dylan and Dakota adored Fallon, and he understood this was a big deal. Enough that he feared her saying no.

She was quiet for so long, his stomach twisted, nerves he rarely experienced suddenly alive inside him. "Your family. The girls. You're not playing around," she said softly.

He lifted one shoulder in a shrug. "I rarely do, as you've so often pointed out. The fact is, I'm finished with any cat-and-mouse games. We already know we're attracted to one another. Let's see where things go." That was as honest as he could be.

"No promises? No games? The minute it's too much for you or the twins, you tell me. And I'll be honest in return. I am not looking for something serious right now but I want to be with you, too. And I adore the girls and would never want to hurt them or give them the wrong impression about us."

Sexual attraction was easy. Feelings were more complicated. Yet how could he not fall for this wary woman when she put his children's feelings before her own?

Reaching out, he grasped her hands. "I want you, Fallon. In my bed and beneath me. On top of me. Every way I can get you."

Her eyes opened wide and she shifted in her seat. "Did that make you uncomfortable? Or aroused?" Okay, he was stepping things up faster than he planned but he didn't want her to have too much time to think and panic. Just feel and agree.

"Aroused," she whispered.

He stroked her cheek and she tipped her head against his hand. "That makes us in agreement," he said, his voice rough with need.

Just talking to her like this had his cock hard in his pants. He was moving them along quickly but she wasn't pulling back. "I promise when we're with the girls, we'll be circumspect so nobody gets hurt. Including and especially you."

She met his gaze, her expression wary. "You seem too good to be true."

"Because you dated a douchebag before me."

She laughed aloud and he liked the sound.

"Now, can you agree to having fun together and no pressure beyond that?" Even if he planned to show her how good things between them could be.

"I can do that," she said, and treated him to a genuine smile, one combined with pleasure, anticipation, and lingering arousal. The same stream of desire he felt rushing through his veins now that he knew they'd taken a huge step forward.

"I'm starving. Want to come back to my apartment? I'm going to pick up Chinese food on the way home. Or do you need to get back to the girls?"

He shook his head. "Liam is going to take them to the burger place we all went to. He wants to rent *Home Alone* for them afterward. They're pretty set until I get home."

Her stomach let out an unladylike rumble and she blushed a pretty shade of pink.

"That's our cue to get going." He rose and held out a hand and she placed her palm in his. Her skin was smooth but a jolt of electricity hit as she curled her fingers around his hand.

They'd most definitely taken a step forward.

Chapter Ten

"*I* *WANT YOU, Fallon. In my bed and beneath me. On top of me. Every way I can get you.*"

No sane woman could turn Noah down. While picking up food, Fallon took the time to think about him and where they were headed. She hadn't invited him to her place just to have dinner. Not when he'd aroused her so thoroughly with his words. Despite her misgivings, she wanted him. Was she really going to let fear override desire because she'd been hurt in the past? She wasn't that naïve young girl anymore, she was a woman with needs.

Agreeing to have sex didn't mean she'd be diving into another ill-advised relationship. Instead, it showed she'd grown up. She was capable of taking control of her life and going after what she wanted. And there was nothing wrong with that.

She had time to see where things led.

Once she met up with Noah at her apartment, instead of the kitchen, she opted for a more relaxed atmosphere and set them up at the family room cocktail table.

Sitting side by side, they devoured the dishes they'd

agreed on, discovering they enjoyed the same things, moderately, but not too spicy food, and soft classical music after a long day. She introduced him to Luciano Pavarotti's collaboration with popular rock musicians as they ate. The food was delicious and soon, she was full of both food and anticipation of what would come next.

She took a sip of water.

From his seat beside her, he stretched his long legs out in front of him. "I can't remember ever having a more relaxing meal." He turned toward her, his hazel gaze focused on her. "Or enjoying better company."

She felt her lips curl in a smile. "Back at you," she said in a voice that was surprisingly low and husky.

Reaching over, he took her glass from her hand and placed it on the table. He leaned close and brushed her hair off her shoulders.

"Noah."

He raised his eyebrows. "Relax, pretty girl." His hand remained resting on her shoulder and he turned his palm toward her face and cupped her cheek. "We're just going to make out for a while."

Her stomach did a flip at his softly spoken words. Words meant to seduce and they were doing their job.

Before she could reply, or even gather her thoughts, his lips grazed hers. Once, then again, before he settled his mouth over hers. The kiss started slow, as if meaning to ease her into it, and she went along willingly, moaning as he traced her lips with his tongue.

She settled her hands on his waist and as she did, he slid a hand into her hair, holding her in place as his seduction turned into more. He parted her mouth, his tongue swooped inside, rubbing against hers, and she tumbled into a world where nothing existed but Noah and his talented kiss. Their tongues tangled together, teeth grazing as need grew.

She didn't know how long they sat making out to the sound of music that suddenly accompanied her to dizzying heights of arousal. How could his kiss make her want so much so fast?

He nipped her bottom lip, the light sting surprising her. Then he soothed the slight pain with his tongue and delved back into the deep recesses of her mouth again and she was lost in sensation once more.

Sometime later, he lifted his head and she realized she lay back against the sofa, Noah's hard body covering hers, the pressure of his arousal pressing insistently between her thighs.

He stared into her eyes, a true smile on his lips.

"God, you should do that more often," she murmured.

He raised one eyebrow. "Do what?"

"Smile." If he hadn't already mesmerized her with

that perfect kiss, the further tilt of his lips would have finished the job.

"I save that part of me for people I care about."

Thump. Thump. Thump. Could he hear her heart beating faster? Because she definitely did.

Was he putting her in that category?

He chuckled but quickly grew more serious. "Yes, that's what I'm saying."

"Are you a mind reader now?" she asked on a shaky breath.

He pushed himself to an upright position and extended a hand, helping her sit up. "I already told you, I'm not asking for anything more than seeing where things between us can go."

He sounded confident they had some kind of future and though she wasn't ready to consider that, he was being honest.

It was exactly what she needed. "I'm willing to try," she said, on a relieved exhale.

Not even her bastard ex, who she had thought she'd been stupidly in love with, cared enough to read her so well. She studied Noah's handsome face, searching for and finding the sincerity in his expression. He was back to stern Noah but not in any way that closed her out.

He rose to his feet and began to gather the dishes and she rushed to stand, not willing to kill the mood further. "Noah, wait."

He set the plates back on the table.

She wrapped her fingers around his hand, her heart pounding in her chest. "I was thinking I could clean up later. I'd rather go back to where we left off, so I can tell you it was the best kiss I ever had." She gathered all her courage because she was about to dive into the deep end.

"It was, was it?" Arrogance snuck into his tone but she figured he deserved to gloat.

"Yes. And can I tell you a secret?"

He raised an eyebrow. "I'm listening."

"I want more of those kisses but not just on my mouth. I need to feel your lips everywhere."

His gaze darkened and he pulled her against him, treating her to a searing hot kiss. One she wouldn't stop, nor would she hesitate again.

Tugging his shirt from his pants, she slid her hands up his warm abdomen. "I know what I want, Noah. And it's you."

THOUGH NOAH FOUND it hard to think with Fallon's small hands on his body, he needed to be sure she hadn't talked herself into something she wasn't ready for.

He understood why she'd panicked earlier. Telling a woman who was skittish about relationships that he cared was akin to lighting a match in a dry forest. He'd seen her expression as panic took hold and there'd been nothing to do except watch her spiral.

"Trust me to know my own mind." Her words penetrated his thoughts. "And let's go back to before," she said, rising onto her tiptoes and brushing her lips over his. "I felt how much you wanted me, and there was never any doubt I wanted you, too." Her hands splayed over his ribs, her touch arousing. "The bedroom is that way." She tilted her head and her hair fell over her shoulder as she waited for his answer.

As if there was anything other than yes. He lifted her into his arms, loving the little squeal of surprise she let out, and carried her into the bedroom.

She'd given him permission and he was ready to go. He lay her down on the bed and began to unbutton his shirt.

"Nope, let me." She tucked her knees beneath her, sat up, and began to unbutton his shirt, letting her nails scrape along his chest as she worked her way down. And once she'd freed the buttons, she pulled his shirt off his shoulders and he dropped it onto the floor.

He glanced down to undo his pants and when he glanced up, she'd shimmied out of her skirt and was in the process of removing her light sweater, leaving herself in a sexy nude bra and barely-there bikini panties.

"Damn, sweetheart. I can't believe I was able to wait so long for you."

Her cheeks turned pink and she smiled, her brown-eyed gaze taking in his bare chest, and the prominent erection protruding from his black boxer briefs. "I'd have to say the same."

Reaching out, he braced his hands on her hips, pulling her close. He lowered himself down so his face was parallel with her flat stomach and the lace panties he wanted off her.

But first… He leaned in and pressed a kiss on her belly. She shivered, grasping his shoulders for support. Working his way down, he left a wet trail down her abdomen until he reached the barrier of clothing. He hooked his thumbs into the sides and pulled the underwear down until it reached her mattress.

"Lay back," he said, his tone gruff.

She raised her arms, and did that easy move women did, and unhooked her bra, letting it fall to the bed. Her breasts were more than a handful with dusky pert nipples that had his mouth watering. But he had another destination to taste first.

She maneuvered herself until she lay back, her legs spread so he could finish what he'd started. He rose to his feet, removed his boxer briefs, then put one knee on the bed. Before he yanked down her panties, he leaned in and took a deep breath, taking in the scent of her arousal. Knowing it was all for him was a heady feeling and he removed the last of her undergarments completely, letting them fall to the floor.

He stared at her naked body for the first time, reminded of her beauty and youth. She wasn't a virgin, thank God, but she was definitely special and someone he wanted to take his time with and savor. Unfortunately, the throbbing of his cock wasn't going to allow for the luxury.

Still, he bent her legs and settled between them, dipping his head for a long, leisurely taste. She moaned as he dove in, gripped his hair, and held on while he brought her to the peak once, lifting his head before she could come and starting over again. He took her to the edge twice more before latching onto her clit and sucking it into his mouth.

Her hips bucked and she tugged at his hair, stinging his scalp. This time he didn't stop. She cried out his name, and he felt like a fucking god as she came and continued to climax, the shudders encompassing her entire body.

He soothed her with his tongue as she collapsed against the mattress and he eased his way up her sweat-sheened body, sealing his lips over hers.

She threaded her fingers through his hair, moaning into his mouth as she wrapped her legs around his waist. He ground his cock against her sex and slid his hands up her sides, capturing her hands above her head.

He'd had his share of partners before but he'd never felt like this about any woman he'd had in his bed. Even if this was *her* bed, the sentiment was the same.

He raised himself off her, meeting her dazed gaze. "So? Was it even better than the best kiss?"

She cupped his face between her hands. "I'll judge after the grand finale."

"I'll take that challenge," he said, and covered her mouth with his.

NOAH KISSED HER, his hands wandering over her body, over her hips, and down her sides. Arousal eased through her, her nipples tightening under his touch. When he rose up, he met her gaze. "Protection," he said in a gruff voice.

She bit down on her lower lip. "I'm on the pill and I haven't been with anyone since my relationship last year. I was tested at my yearly exam," she said, studying his face.

"Can't remember the last time I had sex," he admitted. "Between the girls and work, I don't have much free time. I'm clean as well."

She nodded, relieved at his words. A man like Noah had integrity and she believed him. "I'm good if you are then."

He swallowed hard and nodded. "Inside you bare? Fuck," he muttered. "I'm not sure I'll make it long."

She couldn't hold back her smile. "Might make that challenge hard to live up to." She laughed at her words.

She barely recognized this light version of herself around a man, especially one she was about to have sex with. But Noah made letting go and being real so easy. She could joke and even tease him in ways she'd never done with a guy before.

"You won't be laughing much longer." He bent forward and pulled one of her already sensitive nipples into his mouth, swirling his tongue around the tight bud and grazing it with his teeth.

She moaned, her hips arcing upward as need hit her hard. As if sensing her desire, Noah eased up and wrapped his hand around his impressive erection, thick and ready to enter her. He pumped his shaft, his hand gliding up and down, his gaze never leaving hers.

Her sex grew wet and an emptiness filled her. "Please," she said, ready for him.

He lined himself up at her entrance and nudged his thick cock into her, sliding in and out in slow, steady increments. Leaning forward, he braced his hands beside her head and joined them completely.

"Oh, Noah." Nothing had ever felt as good as Noah Powers. And when he began to move, starting slow and picking up the pace, she saw heaven.

In a shift that shocked her, he rose and settled back on his knees, their bodies still connected. She lifted her legs and bent them back, her hips arching up as her sex clenched around him, and a small sound of pleasure escaped from deep in her throat.

"Hang on," he said, and instinct had her reaching for the slats on the headboard.

He began to move in earnest, thrusting deeper and harder with each pass. He seemed attuned to her, reading her reactions and adjusting his position so his body played hers perfectly, giving her what she needed to soar higher each time he thrust deep.

He drove into her harder and faster and soon she was soaring, seeing stars and a kaleidoscope of brilliant colors. He pumped into her three more times and came hard right after. He released his grip on her legs and collapsed on top of her, his breath now heavy on her neck.

A few minutes later, he rolled off her and she felt him pull out, leaving her feeling empty. On his side, he faced her and she couldn't help but smile.

"Very impressive, Mr. Powers."

He grinned back.

Reaching out, she traced his upward turned lips with her fingertip.

"So? Was that up there with the best kiss ever?" he asked, his tone cocky and sure.

His arrogance was warranted. "I'll give you all three. Best kiss, best oral, and best sex ever."

"Best for me as well." He slid a hand behind her head and pressed a long kiss to her lips. "And something I hope we can repeat."

He broke their connection and rolled to his side, coming to stand by the bed. "I need to shower and get home."

She heard the regret in his tone and wasn't at all hurt or surprised. "Go ahead." She eased the blankets down the bed and slid beneath the covers. "I'll go after you."

"I'd ask you to join me but if I got you naked in the shower I'd never get out of here."

She nodded, pleased with his reply. Once he was closed in the bathroom, she pulled the comforter up to her chin, covering her chilled body.

Alone, she thought about the night, knowing she could do one of two things right now. Dissect what they'd done and panic or enjoy the afterglow. She chose option number two.

Chapter Eleven

NOAH WALKED INTO his apartment in a good mood not even his bickering girls could break. He'd left Fallon with a goodbye kiss meant to ensure she was too dazed to overthink things once he was gone.

"What are they arguing about?" he asked.

"Who talks to Charlie first," his brother said, standing up from the couch and stretching.

He sighed. "Girls! Get in here now."

They ran in, hair in braids, wearing their pajamas. "Daddy!" they each yelled, their default sound.

"Heads or tails?" he asked. "Dakota, it's your turn to choose."

He flipped the coin and she called out, "Heads!"

Sure enough, it landed back in his hand on heads. "Dakota, you talk to your mom first."

"Fine," Dylan said with a pout. "Let's go wait for her to call. The iPad's on my bed."

The girls stomped out and Noah blew out a long breath. "I used to say they could take turns but neither could agree who spoke to her first the last time Charlie called. Hell, half the time I couldn't remember, so I settled on flipping a coin."

His brother chuckled. "They are a handful," he said with fondness in his voice. "I love hanging out with them and I love when I get to give the bickering duo back to you."

"Problem is, when they're not arguing they're plotting."

"Better you than me, bro. At least for now. Good night?"

He nodded, unable to hold back his grin at the thought of having been in Fallon's bed.

"That good? Who is she? The girls were whispering about some chick named Fallon who they wanted to bring to Mom's birthday celebration."

"That's her. Remember the last time the girls ran away?" At Liam's nod, Noah went on. "I found them in an art store where she works. From behind, the twins thought she was Charlie." He shrugged. "Since then, they've been obsessed."

Liam's eyes grew wide. "Seems like they're not the only one. You do realize Mom is going to make a big deal of you bringing someone along with the twins?" They both knew their mother wanted her sons to meet someone and fall hard. She was obvious and vocal about her desire.

"Mom already knows about Fallon. I'm surprised she hasn't mentioned her. Anyway, I told the girls I'd ask her and that's what I went to do today."

"Except you did a lot more than that."

"Isn't it time for you to go home?"

Laughing, Liam scooped up his jacket from the end of the sofa.

Noah walked his sibling to the door and let him out, locking up behind him, then set the alarm. He strode into the kitchen and cleaned up whatever was left for him to do, which mostly involved rinsing the bowl they'd used for popcorn and putting the empty water bottles in the recycling bin.

Shutting the overhead lights, he turned on the lamp in case one of the girls woke up during the night and came to the kitchen for a drink of water, then he peeked into the twins' room to see them talking to their mom. Together. He shook his head at the earlier drama and on his way to his room, he overheard Fallon's name.

It wasn't the first time the twins had mentioned her to Charlie. Which meant it was time for him to discuss his love life with his children's mother. Considering he brought Fallon around the girls often now, he owed it to Charlie to fill her in.

"Daddy!" As if on cue, the girls yelled for him to come take the iPad. Occasionally, Charlie wanted to hear about the girls from him.

He walked in and took the iPad from Dylan.

"Girls, brush your teeth and get ready for bed. I'll be back to tuck you in soon."

He hoped they never outgrew this particular nighttime ritual as it was the favorite part of his day, when the girls were drowsy and quiet and they could talk about anything on their minds.

"Hey, Charlie," he said, bringing the device up so he could see her and vice versa. Walking into his room, he sat down on the bed, mentally preparing for the conversation to come.

"Noah, how are you?" she asked, covering a yawn. She stayed up late to talk to the girls close to their bedtime.

"Busy but good. Yourself?"

"Tired."

Though he wouldn't say as much, she looked exhausted and unhappy. "Are you okay?"

She nodded. "Sometimes living your dream is hard when your other priorities are somewhere else. I miss the girls," she said.

"They miss you too," he assured her.

"Any luck finding a babysitter or nanny?"

He let out a low laugh. "Not at all. And our little terrorists have vowed not to like anyone I bring home."

Charlie raised an eyebrow. "Except Fallon?"

And there it was. As much as he knew he'd have to

bring up the subject, he wasn't surprised she'd gotten to it first. The girls talked about her too often for her not to be curious.

He ran a hand through his hair. "They're... fond of her." She'd already been privy to the explanation of how they'd all met when Noah had insisted they tell their mother about their runaway exploits.

"And so are you?"

He leaned back against the pillows and headboard, and propped the iPad on his raised legs. "And so am I. Listen—"

"No, I want to say something first. Your love life is none of my business except as how—"

"It relates to the girls," he finished for her. "I'd planned to tell you tonight that I'm seeing her and the twins will be around her more often."

Charlie's eyes narrowed and her expression took on what he thought of as her *worried face*. "Is it serious?"

"That's none of your business. She's a good person and adores the twins. She's sensitive to their needs and that's all that should concern you." He had no intention of getting into Fallon's insecurities and past with Charlie. They shared children and that was all.

"Dakota and Dylan said she's coming to your mother's birthday. You're bringing her around your family. Is it so wrong to worry that it's happening fast?

What if you two end things and the girls get hurt?"

He groaned because she made a valid point. But it was one Fallon had already thought of and brought up to him. "I understand and I'll be careful with what I tell the girls about mine and Fallon's relationship." Especially since Fallon was skittish, not that she'd acted it tonight.

Still, once he'd left, he had no doubt her thoughts might spiral. But he was in too deep not to see where things went.

"That's all I ask," Charlie said. "They're our priority."

He bit his tongue when he'd been about to ask if that were really true. The more rational part of him knew she'd had to take this job opportunity, one she'd dreamt about since she'd learned about archeology and digs but in doing so, she'd left the girls with a hole they were trying to fill with Fallon. Not that she was the type to ever try and replace their mom.

"They are a priority," he assured Charlie and they said their goodbyes.

As long as he put the girls' welfare first, Noah had a right to do what made him happy. And Fallon was quickly becoming a key to his happiness. He was lighter when she was around and as she pointed out, he smiled more. Despite the age gap, which he had not told Charlie about, Fallon meant something to him.

Though he understood he needed to take things at her pace, he wasn't about to let her go.

ON SATURDAY MORNING, Fallon stood at her closet door, picking out and discarding clothing on her bed, unhappy with all her choices to wear to meet Noah's family.

As much as she tried to minimize the significance of today's outing and remind herself that Noah said it was a combination of a date and a friend joining them, it was his *parents* and it meant something.

"Breathe," Brooke said from her spot on the bed. She was in the city today and she'd come by to drop off a blouse she'd borrowed and was now helping Fallon choose clothes.

"I'm breathing. It's just that—"

"Nope. It's just a day out with Noah and the girls. It's not like you have an audience with the King of England." She let out an amused laugh at her own joke.

Fallon rolled her eyes. "Like you've never gotten fussy about what to wear when my brother shows up in town."

"Rude," she muttered, but she was blushing and still half smiling and therefore not really mad. She grabbed a pillow from the other side of the bed and repositioned herself so she was more comfortable. Then she pointed to the corner of the bed. "Wear that skirt."

Fallon picked up the black pleated skirt on the top of the pile. "This one?"

Brooke nodded. "And this top." She lifted a light blue sweater that would look perfect with the skirt. "Add a pair of black short boots and your cute leather jacket." She slid off the bed and stood. "And my job here is done." She took a bow for her effort.

"Thank you!" Fallon hung the garment over her arm and walked over to hug her friend. "You're the best."

"I try. But seriously, relax and be yourself. Whatever this thing is between you and Noah, his family will love you. How could they not? You're a sweetheart. And you saved the girls from the big city. Now go, have fun, and for the love of God, *don't think*!"

Laughing, Fallon walked her friend to the door and let her out, promising to text her and let her know how things went.

She showered and dressed in the outfit Brooke picked out, then put on a light layer of makeup, being true to herself. She decided to wear her hair in a bun with soft tendrils framing her face.

When Noah called to say he and the girls were in

the car downstairs, she picked up the gift she'd wrapped for his mom, drew a deep breath, and walked out her door.

She took the elevator downstairs, said hello to her doorman, and stepped into the cooler air. Noah stood by the passenger door.

"Hi!" she said as she joined him.

"Hi, yourself." His hazel eyes appeared more green than brown in the sunlight, helped along by his hunter-colored thermal shirt. She wanted to devour him whole and had to remind herself the twins were in the back seat.

"You look beautiful," he said, gesturing for her to have a seat.

"You're pretty handsome yourself, Mr. Powers."

He let out a low growl and she thought it was prudent to break the sexual tension and get into the car.

She eased into the vehicle, then turned around and smiled. "Hi, girls!"

"Hi, Fallon!" they chimed in unison.

Noah settled into the driver's seat and soon they were on their way.

"What's in the box you're holding?" Dylan asked.

She laughed. "Can it be a surprise present for your grandmother?"

"You didn't have to do that but it was sweet," Noah said. "Girls, you can be surprised along with

125

Grandma Nina."

"Boo," Dylan said.

Dakota let out a loud huff.

"Ignore them," he said. "But you can whisper what it is in my ear."

"Dad!" they shrieked.

"Kidding!" His mouth quirked up in a grin. The same mouth that had done dirty things to her just a couple of days ago, she thought, and immediately began squirming in her seat.

"Are you okay?" he asked.

She smoothed her hand over her skirt and nodded. "Yep. Never better."

Reaching over, he took her hand and held it on the ride to Greenwich, CT, where his parents resided. All the while she told herself to enjoy and instructed herself *not* to think. At all.

Chapter Twelve

NOAH PULLED INTO the long driveway surrounded by tall trees leading to his parents' house. They'd moved to the white clapboard colonial-styled home after his father had retired from his career as a lawyer and became a federal court judge. While growing up in nearby Westchester, New York, his mother had stayed home with the kids, donating her time to charity and being a class-mom presence for her children throughout the years.

As they reached the front door, he noticed Fallon visibly draw in a nervous breath and he reached for her hand, squeezing in reassurance. "I promise they don't bite."

The front door opened before she could reply and the twins hugged their grandparents, then raced inside where no doubt his mom had whispered she had homemade chocolate chip cookies in the kitchen.

They all stepped inside and Noah began introductions. "Mom, Dad, I'd like you to meet Fallon Sterling. Fallon, my parents, Nina and Joseph Powers."

"So nice to meet you," his father said, enclosing Fallon's small hand in his.

"It's a pleasure," she said. "Happy Birthday, Mrs. Powers." She held out her gift and his mom took it from her hands.

"Thank you, Fallon. So unnecessary but very sweet. Welcome! Come, let's go to the kitchen. I have warm cookies… if the girls left any for us."

"Where is everyone else?" Noah asked, following them to the noisy room where his girls were talking loudly.

"Shannon and the boys should be here any minute." She ushered them around the center island where the twins already sat next to each other and were, predictably, munching on cookies.

"Girls, leave room for lunch and cake," Noah said.

His mother placed Fallon's gift on a side counter and walked up beside her. For the next twenty minutes, the women chatted, his mother asking questions about Fallon's career and art, which they'd heard about from the twins. She seemed genuinely interested, so he turned his focus to his father and they caught up until the doorbell rang.

His mother rushed to answer it and Noah used this time to sidle up to Fallon. "How are you doing?" he asked.

"Good. Your mother is so warm and sweet," she said with a hint of melancholy in her tone. Before he could question her, she said, "She reminds me a little

128

of my mom."

And he knew immediately she was missing her own mom. He put his arm around her waist and pulled her close, kissing the side of her forehead. "I want to know more about her," he said.

She nodded just as his siblings entered the room en masse and the chaos began. The rest of the day passed with the same friendly vibe from his siblings, who welcomed Fallon easily. Since she'd already met Shannon, they talked for a while. Liam and Simon paid her a good deal of attention and he knew for certain she fit into his family.

Especially when, after cake, the gifts were opened. His mom picked up Fallon's midway through the pile of presents. She cut the ribbon and ripped open the paper, pulling out a 5x7 picture frame.

She glanced at the photo and a huge smile lit up her face. "This is perfect! Thank you! Look, everyone!" she said and turned the frame around so everyone could see.

"That's us!" Dakota exclaimed.

In the center of the intricate silver lace-looking design was a photo of the twins the day they'd painted their pictures at the studio. Each girl smiled wide as they held up the unicorns they'd painted, which now hung in their room. Dakota had a streak of pink paint on one cheek and Dylan was pointing at the unicorn with one finger. Fallon had captured their elation from the day perfectly.

"I remember you taking that," Dylan said.

At the thoughtful gift, a lump rose in Noah's throat. Not only had Fallon brought his mom a gift but it had been well considered and exactly what his mother would love. He wished he wasn't across the room from her so he could squeeze her hand or let her know how much the gesture meant to him.

"Fallon, this is perfect. Really. I'll put it up by my side of the bed." She said the last part more to herself than anyone else.

"I wanted to paint an elephant but Fallon didn't have any as examples," Dakota said. "Hey! Did you know they used to 'xecute people by having elephants sit on them?" she asked.

Execute, he thought as the room went silent at her fact spouting. He loved how much she learned about ancient civilizations thanks to her mother, but he wished the information wasn't always so... gruesome.

"That's fascinating, honey. Okay, next gift," Noah said, breaking the silence and shooting his brother Simon, who was about to laugh, a warning look.

His mother cleared her throat and went back to opening gifts. Once she'd finished, Fallon and Shannon insisted on helping with cleanup, throwing out all the wrapping paper and straightening up the kitchen.

Noah excused himself to take a call from one of the associates in his law firm who was working over the weekend and when he returned, his brothers were gathered around the leftover cake with the girls, who were eating an extra piece. That made him glad they were staying with his parents tonight. At least he wouldn't have to get them to sleep while on a sugar high.

Shannon and his mother were talking in the corner and he'd passed his father, who'd dozed off in the recliner in the family room. Bless the man, he could sleep through the girls' excitement and shrieking. Probably came from having three rambunctious sons and one outgoing daughter.

Looking around for Fallon, he found her looking out the sliding glass doors in the kitchen which showcased the view of his parents' large yard. A pool, an old wooden swing set he and his siblings had used, and a beautiful sitting area under a gazebo.

He walked up behind her and put his arms around her waist, his chin on her shoulder. "Beautiful, isn't it?"

She nodded. "You and your siblings must have had a blast playing outside when you were younger."

"We did. The girls love it now." He brushed her hair off her shoulder and whispered, "Did I mention they're sleeping here tonight?"

A shiver racked her body and she leaned back against him. "I did notice their duffel bags."

"So… your place or mine?" he asked.

"I—" Her words were cut off by the sound of a phone ringing. "That's mine." She slipped her hand into a pocket in her skirt, pulled out her cell, and glanced at it. "It's Clara." She slid her thumb across the screen and took the call. "Hello, Clara."

Because he stood so close, he could hear the conversation.

"Hello, dear. I'm sorry to bother you but I'm at the gallery and I'm not feeling well. I can't reach Oliver and I'm worried," she said, lowering her voice.

Fallon's body stiffened and she turned to Noah. "I need to go to her."

He nodded, knowing how close she felt to her boss and mentor. "Why don't you have her call 911, find out what hospital they're taking her to, and we can meet her there?"

"You should stay with your family, I can take a rideshare."

He shook his head. "Not happening."

She shot him a grateful look, her gaze softening, then returned to the call and repeated what he'd said to Clara.

They said their goodbyes to the family, calmed the girls, assuring them Clara was a friend of Fallon's and she'd be fine, and they were off.

Fallon was silent on the ride to the city, her worry for Clara causing her foot to tap while drumming her nails on the leather on the door.

Though he attempted to join Fallon inside the ER, he wasn't family and they only wanted one person at a time. After claiming to be Clara's daughter, she was allowed in.

She paused to talk to him first. "I don't know how long I'll be here, so you should go home. I can take an Uber home." She rushed off to see Clara before he could reply.

He had no intention of leaving her to come out alone later. So Noah settled in to wait.

Chapter Thirteen

FALLON WAS DIRECTED to a cubicle with a sliding door to which Clara had been assigned. Her boss lay back in bed, her skin pale, oxygen being given to her through the small cannula in her nose.

"Clara, I'm here. I'd have come sooner but I wasn't in the city. How are you?" Fallon pulled a chair over to the bed, lifted Clara's hand, and held it between her palms.

"I was dizzy and out of breath. Oliver said he tried to get me an appointment with a specialist but there were no openings for six weeks. He said I should go to work and it would be mind over matter. I'd feel better being busy."

Fallon clenched her teeth. Sylvie was supposed to work today and she was bringing a friend to train.

But what was wrong with Oliver? Was he trying to work his mother to death? "Oh, Clara. I wish you'd called me sooner."

"Sylvie was working with her friend, so I had help. I was able to relax at my desk. But the shortness of breath returned when I wasn't exerting myself and it frightened me."

"What are they doing for you?" she asked, gently holding her hand as she met her gaze.

Clara's blue eyes appeared cloudy. "They are doing blood tests to see if I had a heart attack and they want to run some other tests too. They explained them but I'm so tired I didn't process much of what they said."

Clara's son should have been there to bring his mother to the hospital and play interpreter with the doctors. "Where is Oliver?" Fallon asked.

"He said he had an important meeting but I left a message on his phone that I was here. I'm sure he'll come rushing in any moment."

Fallon had her doubts.

"Fallon, while we're alone, I wanted to talk to you."

"Of course," Fallon said, leaning forward. "What can I do for you?"

Clara cleared her throat. "I spoke to my lawyer about my will."

"Your *will*? Clara, please. Don't dwell on that." Nobody liked thinking about death, but Fallon hated it from personal experience. She shuddered at the memories that came back and focused on Clara.

Reaching up, the other woman removed the oxygen from her nose, probably so she could speak more clearly. "It's prudent for someone of my means to think ahead. And when I wasn't feeling well it made me start thinking and act on what's important."

Not wanting to think about a world without Clara in it, Fallon swallowed over the lump in her throat. Just the idea reminded her of the gaping loss of her mother. Her father and brothers had tried hard to compensate, as did Lizzie, but a little girl needed her mom.

"Okay," she said, aware of how important this topic was to Clara. "What about your will?"

"Darling, should something happen to me, I am leaving you the gallery."

She gasped, shock rendering her mute.

"Don't look so surprised. Nobody loves the place like I do… except you. I want it to go to someone who loves art, knows how to stock it, and sell beautiful things to people who will enjoy them. Nobody does that as well as you. Not even me."

A tear fell from her eye and she wiped it with the back of her hand. "I don't know what to say."

"Say you'll give the place all the love you do now and I'll be happy."

Still at a loss for words, she nodded and managed to whisper, "I promise. Now please put the oxygen back?"

Clara smiled and did as she asked, reseating the oxygen, allowing Fallon to relax that she could breathe easier.

"Mother!" Oliver came barging into the room, rushing to his mother's side, and all but pushing Fallon out of the way. "I was tied up in a meeting and just got your message. I'm so sorry I wasn't there for you."

"Oliver! Apologize for shoving Fallon aside," Clara said.

He turned to face her with cold eyes. "My apologies." He pivoted to face his mother. "I told you to try not to think about things. You probably have indigestion. What do the doctors say?"

"They're testing for a heart attack," Fallon told him through gritted teeth. "Clara, do whatever tests they want you to do."

Aware Oliver had taken over and she was no longer needed here, Fallon stepped across the room to the other side of the bed.

"I'm going to leave you two alone." Leaning down, she kissed the other woman's cheek. "Feel better. I'll call and check on you tonight. Maybe you'll have news from the doctors." She glanced around the room, her gaze landing on Clara's cell. Do you have your phone charger?"

Clara shook her head.

"Well, I happen to carry an extra." Fallon retrieved it from her bag and plugged it into the wall, aware of Oliver's calculating stare as she hooked up Clara's cell. "Talk to you later."

She walked out in a state of shock from Clara's pronouncement, heading out through the waiting room of the ER.

"Fallon!"

She turned at the sound of Noah's voice, surprised he was still waiting. "Noah! You stayed."

"You rushed off before I could let you know I was waiting until you were through."

She leapt forward and wrapped her arms around his neck, pulling him into a hug. "Thank you." She wasn't ashamed to admit she needed him. "I have a lot to tell you."

He slid a hand into hers. "Then let's go back to my place, which you've never seen, and we can talk."

Chapter Fourteen

"I INTEND TO take you on a real date one of these days," Noah said, as they settled onto his large sofa. They'd cleaned up from an ordered-in Italian dinner which they'd eaten while also enjoying a bold, red wine.

She smiled. "I'd love that," she murmured.

But she seemed subdued and preoccupied, and though he assumed she was worried about Clara, he wondered if there wasn't something more going on. Not wanting to push right away, he steered the conversation to his mom's birthday, the twins' love of cake, and he complimented Fallon on the gift she'd bought for his mother. It definitely topped the robe he'd bought as his present.

He waited until Fallon had eaten and consumed enough wine to relax her before turning to more serious topics. "How is Clara?" he asked.

Fallon raised one shoulder and lowered it again. "I'm not sure. She looks pale and tired, and they're running tests. I left because her son was there, but frankly he's useless. He doesn't care about his mother unless she's lending him money." Little worry lines creased between her eyes.

"I'm sorry," he said. "I know how much you care about her." He leaned against the sofa cushion and pulled Fallon with him, wrapping an arm around her shoulders.

With a sigh, she leaned her head against him. "Today was hard. Clara started talking about revising her will." Her voice grew shaky and he understood how difficult the subject was for her.

"I'm here and I'm listening," he said.

She pushed herself away and turned to face him. "She said she's leaving me the gallery! And I didn't know what to say. I mean, she has a son who she could give her business to, but she said she knows how much I love it and that I'll pass on that love to people who come in to shop."

"What a generous thing to do," he said, as surprised as Fallon seemed to be.

She nodded. "I've always wanted my own gallery and she knew that. I do have a trust fund that I could use to open my own business, but I wanted to soak up as much knowledge as I could from Clara before I acted to fulfill that dream. I know how fortunate I am and I didn't want to just open a gallery only to have to close it again because I hadn't done my due diligence."

"Smart of you," he murmured, admiring her intelligence and ability to see past just having the money.

He operated his life the same way.

Tears filled her eyes and he wiped at her damp cheek. "Happy tears?" he asked.

"A combination. I don't like to think of Clara dying." She visibly swallowed hard. "It reminds me of losing my mother."

He sighed, feeling her pain. "You never told me what happened to her." Reaching out, he took her hand, hoping their connection would allow her to trust him.

She glanced down, then met his gaze. "I was ten when it happened. My father owns an investment firm and he had a client that directed Dad's investments, then blamed him when he lost a lot of money. Dad had tried to warn him but he believed the stocks would turn around."

He waited in silence, letting her gather her thoughts.

She cleared her throat. "Anyway, one night over the summer, Dad was out at a business dinner and I was sleeping upstairs. Aiden, Jared, and Dex were at summer camp. Remy was seventeen and he'd stayed home." Her voice shook as she spoke and he stroked his thumb over the top of her hand.

"Take your time," he said, waiting patiently.

She blew out a breath and nodded, indicating she was ready again. "Remy was supposed to take Mom and me out for dinner but some girl he liked called and wanted to see him, so he blew us off." Her lips lifted in a wry smile. "I remember being so annoyed at the time. But then Mom and I ordered in and watched a movie, and after, I went to my bed to sleep."

She paused and Noah braced himself for... he didn't know what. "Dad's client broke into the house and shot my mother. He was punishing my dad for his business losses. He killed her while I was upstairs sleeping." She sniffed and the tears fell from her eyes.

"Oh, sweetheart. I'm so sorry." Noah held out his arms and she burrowed in, settling in his lap to accept his comfort. Sliding a hand up the back of her shirt, he rubbed slow circles, calming her as she cried.

After a while, she hiccupped and pulled back, her eyes red but she was no less beautiful to him.

"No matter how much time passes, when I talk about her, it still feels as painfully fresh as when it happened."

"You were a little girl. You understand so much more now. It must be like reliving the loss."

She nodded. Blinked. And more moisture leaked from her eyes. "I'm sorry," she said, rubbing her eyes with the arm of her sweater.

"For what? Getting emotional? Please. I'm just glad you feel like you can let go with me."

She tipped her head, studying him, as if seeing him

for the first time. "I do," she said, surprise in her voice.

She moved to him, placed her hands on his shoulders, and sealed her lips over his.

His desire to comfort her was as strong as his physical need. Pulling her against him, he slid a hand into her hair, cupping her head and deepening the kiss.

Chapter Fifteen

AFTER TELLING THE story of her mother's murder, Fallon needed to get lost in Noah and he was there, his big strong arms wrapping around her and positioning her more securely in his lap. Her sex sat on his hard cock and one rock had a wave of pleasure rolling through her.

Desperate for an escape from the memories, she focused on Noah. Sliding her hands between their bodies, she pulled up the shirt he wore and pressed her palms against his warm, hard stomach. The difference between her softer body and his rock-hard one was arousing and she ran her hands up his chest until she covered his nipples, pausing long enough to rub each one between her thumb and forefinger.

A low rumble escaped from deep inside him and before she knew it, he'd risen from the sofa with her in his arms. She locked her ankles around his back while he walked them to the bedroom, all the while kissing her and nipping at her jaw.

He deposited her on the mattress and stared down at her, his gaze almost feral, and said, "Naked. Now." The barked two-word command seemed to be the only words he could manage as his hands went to his pants button and he began to follow his own orders.

Not wanting to wait a moment to join him, Fallon quickly removed the skirt and panties. Socks next. Her shoes she'd already left by the front entrance. Naked from the bottom down, with one hand she pulled off her shirt and met him as an equal.

His gloriously naked body had her sex turning wet with need and she reached out to encircle his cock with her hand. She slid her palm over the hot, hard flesh and she let out a moan of need.

She slid off the bed and sunk to her knees on the plush carpeted floor. His heavy-lidded gaze never left hers as she licked the head of his erection, eliciting a full-body shudder from Noah. Then she replaced her hand with her mouth, pulling him between her lips as deep as she could manage.

His hand came to rest on top of her head, his body stiff as she gazed up at him, looking for a sign. Of what, she didn't know, but when his eyes warmed from hazel green to a deeper brown, she licked underneath of his shaft, swirling her tongue around the top and tasting the precum at the tip.

"Fuck," he ground out, only to shift his hips and begin a slow and steady thrusting motion.

She felt him hold back, not going as deep as she assumed he both needed and wanted. Reaching a hand down, she tried to pinch his thigh as a sign but the taut skin was hard and tight.

He glanced at her. "Do you want more, sweet girl?"

She nodded.

"You're sure you can take more?"

Again, she treated him to a small bob of her head.

Her agreement worked like a release valve and he went from slow and measured to faster, never taking his gaze from hers, obviously judging how much she could handle. And she was determined to take what he gave.

His movements picked up and soon she was at his mercy, his cock hitting the back of her mouth with every repeat thrust. Her eyes watered and she gagged a few times, at which point he'd slow down, check on her, and return to where they'd been.

With one hand, she braced herself on his thigh, with the other, she cupped his balls and tugged lightly. His hips moved faster and his thrusts became less smooth, more jerky until he stiffened and came with a loud groan, followed by her name on his lips.

She swallowed what she could and somehow rose and stumbled to the bathroom to fix herself. Next thing she knew, he'd joined her in the bathroom, hefted her over his shoulder so she squealed, and flopped her down on the bed.

He came over her and thrust deep. The man had stamina because he was rock hard and ready to go again, taking her hard and sending her soaring before she had a chance to catch her breath.

A long time later, Noah held her in his arms. Her thoughts were quiet, her breathing now slow and steady. And as she drifted off, she realized she felt safe with him and after tonight, closer than ever before.

FALLON WOKE TO the sun streaming through the blinds, the covers kicked low so they covered only her bare bottom. With a sigh, she stretched, feeling the delicious pull of rarely used muscles as she slowly came awake and began to process her thoughts.

Noah lay beside her and she turned her head to find him watching her. "C'mere," he said, and she scooted closer.

He propped himself up against the pillows and she nested in the crook of his shoulder as he wrapped his arm around her waist.

"Morning," he rumbled, once he had her positioned where he wanted her.

She couldn't help but smile. "Morning." She lay her head on his chest, soaking in his warmth.

"What's on your agenda for today?" he asked,

twirling her hair in his finger.

"Well, I have to be at work around noon, but we have help now, so I feel a little more flexible and less panicked. I would like to check on Clara. Other than that, not much. How about you?"

"I am going to take advantage of my free morning before I have to go get the twins and catch up on some paperwork."

"And after?"

"I thought if the forecast is still on the warmer side, I'd ask the girls if they want to go to the zoo. Give Dakota some time to spout her little-known facts about certain species," he said with a chuckle.

She smiled, then splayed her hand on his chest. "You're such a good dad."

"It wasn't easy at first," he murmured. "But you know what they say, parenting doesn't come with a manual. You get thrown into the deep end and you have no choice but to swim because that baby relies on you for everything."

"Or in your case, babies, plural."

He let out a chuckle. "True. But then they become little people with personalities, and it's easier to know what might make them happy."

"Like the zoo."

"Like the zoo," he agreed. He grew quiet and she left him to his thoughts but the silence became prolonged.

"What are you thinking about?" she asked.

He lifted the other shoulder. "Just that these are the things their mother is missing out on. Taking them to the zoo. Going ice skating in Central Park closer to the holidays. And if she's missing out, so are the girls."

Fallon sighed. "I can't say I know what it's like to be a mom." Though she hoped to one day. "But I imagine she's torn between a once-in-a-lifetime opportunity to follow her dreams, and the twins. I've never met her but Dakota and Dylan are very well-adjusted kids. That's due to your joint parenting. Everyone will be fine," she assured him.

"Anyone ever tell you you're pretty wise for some-one so young?"

"My brothers call me a wise-ass, does that count?"

He chuckled and they settled back into their own thoughts, leaving Fallon to realize he'd confided in her about his fears for the girls. Oh, he'd mentioned it before, but she'd heard the deeper worry behind the words and was grateful she could be here to soothe his concerns, something Ezra had never let her do.

He'd pat her on the head and minimize her own worries but he never confided in her about his deepest feelings. Noah's ability to tap into his emotions and be vulnerable made him more of a stand-up guy than anyone she'd known in the past. Definitely more than her ex. Noah Powers was his own man and she appreciated everything about him.

They must have dozed back to sleep because she woke again, this time to the ringing of her cell phone in the other room.

"I'll grab it." Noah levered his big body up and strode out of room, unabashedly nude.

She took the time to admire the view.

"Like what you see?" he asked with a smirk on his handsome face. Even with bedhead and a scruff of beard on his face, he was the best-looking man she'd ever seen.

"I take the Fifth. Your ego is big enough."

He tossed the phone onto the bed and she picked it up and glanced at the screen. She didn't recognize the number but the message left made her freeze.

"What's wrong?"

"It was the police. The gallery was vandalized," she said, already scrambling out of bed, her mind on the valuable, irreplaceable artwork inside.

"Jump in the shower, I'll be right there. Then I'll take you over."

Shivering and numb, she did as Noah suggested, taking a quick shower, then ceding the bathroom to him. All the while she was grateful that however bad this was, she wouldn't have to face it alone.

★ ★ ★

NOAH DROVE THEM to the gallery and parked in a spot across the street. Yellow police tape prevented them from entering. Fallon approached the officer on duty and explained she worked there.

He let them walk inside.

"Oh my God!" Fallon placed a hand over her open mouth, horror dripping from her words as she took in the scene.

Noah wrapped an arm around her waist and led her to one of the barstools set up in the corner. She sat down, her breathing heavy, as she obviously tried to come to terms with the destruction.

"Oliver!" she exclaimed, and jumped out of her seat.

Noah turned and caught sight of Clara's son walking toward them.

"Fallon. How did you know to be here?" he asked, folding his arms across his chest.

"I'm on the emergency list. Where's Clara?"

"Right here," her boss said, as she slowly made her way from the back room.

Even from a distance, Noah could see the dark circles under her eyes and the wan appearance of her skin. Even Noah realized the older woman had gone downhill fast.

"Clara, come sit." Fallon rushed over and with the aid of her walker, helped Clara to sit. "Why didn't you send Oliver? You need to be in bed!"

"She insisted on coming," Oliver said.

"Fallon, look at the destruction." Tears were in the other woman's eyes.

Fallon rubbed her back. "Was anything stolen?"

"The police asked me to take inventory and do a list. I assured him we'd get that done as soon as possible. But at a glance, it doesn't appear that way."

Noah narrowed his gaze. "That's odd."

"Is it?" Oliver asked. "Today's youth is callous and lacks appreciation for the finer things."

Clara remained silent and Fallon glanced away but not before Noah noticed her hand curl into a fist at his elitist words and snooty tone.

Fallon clasped Clara's hand. "Everything is in-sured. It's going to be okay."

"Frankly, I think my mother's had it. This gallery is a burden to her in her fragile state. I can help you shut down—"

"Oliver!" Clara managed to snap at her son. "That is not happening. Fallon is more than capable of putting things to rights here, seeing what was de-stroyed or taken, and contacting the artists. I will call the insurance company when I get home. I told you this gallery means everything to me. You will not

155

discuss taking it away from me again."

With a good old-fashioned *harrumph*, he stormed off in the direction of the office and Noah wanted to applaud the effort it took for Clara to stand up to her son.

"Ms. Morganville, can I get you something? A cup of tea?" Noah offered, and Fallon treated him to a grateful smile.

She shook her head. "Oliver has been bringing me tea constantly. I think I could float away." She shook her head and managed a laugh. "And please, call me Clara."

"Yes, ma'am," he said.

"Fallon, we're going to have to close down while we get the place fixed up and find out how soon we can get more inventory."

Fallon nodded. "I know. I'll take care of every-thing. If you're up to it, just handle the insurance since it's in your name. After that, you rest. I've got things handled here."

"Thank you, darling girl. I can trust you have my best interests at heart." With a smile, Clara pushed herself out of the seat.

Noah jumped up but let her have her dignity as she stood. He was there should she fall. Then, Fallon made small talk so she could accompany Clara to the back office.

By the time she reemerged, Oliver had a hand under his mother's elbow and was escorting her outside to his car.

Fallon stood by Noah, watching the duo. She sighed. "I don't understand how she's so sick so suddenly."

"Did you talk to her about seeing a specialist?" he asked.

"Every time I do, it seems like Oliver shows up, reassuring me he's taking care of his mother." She frowned and sighed, glancing around the gallery. "Oh, my painting was damaged!" Fallon exclaimed. "I should have pulled it off the wall since I had every intention of surprising the girls with it." Frustrated tears filled her gaze.

"Hey. There's nothing we can do here, so let's go. The longer you stay looking at the vandalism, the more upset you'll get."

"Okay." She treated him to a smile he knew was forced. "You can take me home and go pick up the girls from your parents."

He raised an eyebrow. "First, my parents are bringing them home to me, and second, I'm not sending you home alone when you're upset. I can guarantee the girls will be happy to take your mind off the break-in, at least for a little while."

She wrapped her arms around his neck and held

him tight. "Thank you. I really didn't want to be by myself."

With a brighter look in her eyes, they shut the lights and walked out, checking in with the officers outside before they left.

Chapter Sixteen

FALLON SAT IN the kitchen in Noah's apartment, a modern space with white cabinets and black quartz countertops with white veining running through. Definitely a good choice for two active girls who probably liked to make a mess.

Noah had excused himself to take a work call. Despite it being the weekend, a lawyer's life didn't lend itself to nine-to-five hours. Still, she felt calmer here than she would have in her apartment, pacing and worrying, and was grateful Noah had offered her sanctuary here. She'd have to deal with the reality of working through the damage soon enough. She'd already made a list of artists to contact, knowing she'd add to it when she returned to the gallery and was able to access the computer there.

She wrapped her hands around a mug filled with coffee and took a long sip, sadness filling her at the loss of all the beautiful, one-of-a-kind art that had been destroyed. And for what? Someone who got a kick out of breaking in and getting away with it? She hoped the cameras in the gallery picked up something useful for the police, who'd mentioned Clara had given them access and they would be in touch once they sent the information to their tech people.

"Daddy! We're home!" one of the twins screamed.

Her lips lifted and she laughed. She hadn't heard anyone enter. Then again, this apartment was massive and she wasn't anywhere near the front entrance.

The twins came to a skidding halt in the kitchen and when they noticed Fallon, Dylan shrieked. "Grandma, Fallon's here!"

Nina walked into the room, a smile on her face. "I can see that. No need to break my eardrums."

"Fallon! We watched a show on National Geographic with Grandpa. Did you know that rhinocerhouses talk to each other with their poop?" Dakota asked.

Dylan giggled at her sister's words.

"If they mark their spots, other rhinocerhouses know not to go there and they don't get into a fight."

Fallon blinked at the information, as usual, at a loss as to what to say to the young, quite brilliant girl.

"That's rhinoceroses. It's the plural for more than one rhino," Noah's dad said, joining them in the kitchen. "And hello, Fallon."

His mom treated her to a warm smile.

"Hi, Mr. and Mrs. Powers."

His mom waved a hand through the air. "Nina and Joseph, remember?"

Fallon nodded and smiled.

"Where's Daddy?" Dakota asked.

"He's in his office but he should be out soon. I had a little…" She glanced at the girls before meeting Nina's gaze. "Excitement at the gallery and he offered to let me hang out here for the day." She felt the need to explain her reason for being here. The last thing she'd want was for his parents to think they'd spent the night together, even if they had.

The sound of heavy footsteps treading across the apartment caught Fallon's attention and Noah strode into the room, his T-shirt showing his powerful forearms and despite, or rather, because of his casual look, her mouth watered at the sight of him.

"Did I hear a herd of elephants in here?" Noah asked, opening his arms so the twins could run into them.

The sight warmed her heart. She adored how much the twins loved their father, testament to what a spectacular job he was doing raising them alone.

Feeling the heat of someone's gaze, she turned to see Nina watching her watch the scene, a speculative look in her eyes, and Fallon's stomach twisted with nerves. She just wanted his mother to like her.

"Funny you should mention elephants," Fallon said in an effort to switch the other woman's focus.

"Yeah, we watched a show with Grandpa!" Dylan said.

Dakota went into her rhino poop information, mispronunciations and all, and soon, everyone was laughing and Nina Powers was no longer watching Fallon stare at the small family with what had probably been longing in her gaze.

His parents stayed for an hour and they'd moved to the family room, relaxing and talking before leaving to see a matinee on Broadway.

As soon as goodbyes had been said and Noah walked his parents out, the girls surrounded her. "Can we do mani-pedis?" Dylan asked. "I have a manicure set!" she exclaimed.

Dakota wrinkled her nose. "Nooo! It's so boring."

If Fallon had to guess, she couldn't sit still long enough for the process. "Well, that's up to your dad. Dakota, why don't you think about something fun I can paint on your nails just in case we do them?" She figured that would entice the girl to agree with her sister's desire.

"Oooh! Rhino poop!" She giggled, grabbing her stomach and dropping to the floor, rolling with laughter at her own joke.

"What's so funny?" Noah asked, as he returned to the family room.

"Don't ask, Dad. Just don't ask." Dylan walked up to her father and clasped both hands in front of her.

"What do you want?" he asked, sounding pre-resigned to not liking the answer.

Dakota jumped up from her theatrics on the floor. "Can Fallon give us mani-pedis, Daddy? Please?"

"Please?" Dylan chimed in, hands still clasped in prayer.

He immediately shook his head. "Girls, Fallon's had a rough—I mean busy morning. We don't need to bother her."

"It's no bother. They're an amazing distraction. Besides, I said I'd paint something special on Dakota's nails."

"Not poop!" Dylan shrieked.

He wrinkled his nose. "I really don't want to know." Glancing at Fallon, he mouthed, *Are you sure?* She nodded, suddenly looking forward to a spa day with Noah's girls.

He shot her a grateful look. "Then I will disappear into my office and get some work done. Girls, make sure you help Fallon clean up afterward," he said in his stern dad voice.

One she wasn't ashamed to admit turned her on despite their young audience.

EVEN SECLUDED IN his office, Noah heard the girlish shrieks and laughter from the kitchen. He'd stopped by the room for a glass of water and had been shocked to see the twins soaking their toes in plastic containers filled with soapy water.

They barely noticed him, lost in their excitement and chatter. He couldn't remember the last time he'd seen the girls so animated and happy. In fact, he'd never seen Fallon so engrossed in something to the exclusion of all else, including him. And he couldn't express the warmth that filled him, knowing this young woman—and she was young—truly loved spending time with his girls. Not to impress him, not as a means to get closer to him, but because the twins made her as happy as they made him.

He snuck out of the kitchen, happy to be invisible, and returned to his office where he worked to the sound of joy and fun filling both his apartment and his heart.

He didn't know how much time had passed when a knock sounded on his office door. He glanced up to see Fallon hovering in the doorway, seemingly unsure if she should enter.

He gestured for her to come in and she strode across the hardwood floor, coming to a stop across from him.

"Closer," he said, indicating she should walk around the large desk.

She did as instructed, coming around to his side.

"Where are the girls?" he asked.

She laughed. "I took the mini fans from their rooms and told them to sit in front of the fans to let their nails dry."

"Brilliant," he said, as he pulled her onto his lap.

"We shouldn't!"

"I'll hear them coming. Trust me."

She bit down on her enticing lower lip and nodded. "I do."

Why did those little words do such crazy things to his heart rate? "It sounded like you were having fun."

"They're amazing girls. I love getting to learn their different personalities." She waved a hand through the air and he caught her wrist in his hand.

Her fingers were different colors, one hand hot pink and blue, the other purple and orange, none of which were within the shape of her nails. The polish extended onto her fingers.

"You let them paint your nails," he said, staring at the mess in disbelief.

"Of course. It's just polish."

"This hand is Dakota and this is Dylan's handiwork." She held up each hand for him to see.

Releasing her hand, he pressed a palm to her cheeks. "You, Fallon Sterling, are a true treasure." He leaned forward and captured her lips with his.

He put all the emotion into the kiss he couldn't express in words. How much he liked her, admired her, appreciated her. With every swipe of their tongues, his cock grew harder and she squirmed in his lap, breaking the kiss before he was ready.

"Not while the girls are in the other room," she said, hopping up from her seat.

She was right and he released her. "I had fun today. It was definitely the distraction I needed before facing the hard day tomorrow."

"Work?"

She nodded. "Cataloguing the destruction. It shouldn't take me long. I'm familiar with the art. It just breaks my heart to see the callousness in the world. And I dread calling the artists."

"I understand."

"About the twins, I had an idea. Once I handle all the gallery work, which shouldn't take longer than half a day tomorrow, I'm off until Clara has the walls repainted and gets the place ready to open again."

As if they knew they were the subject of conversation, the thud of their bare feet came padding toward the office.

"Why don't I watch the twins while I'm off?" she asked, just as their identical faces appeared in the doorway.

"Fallon's going to be our nanny!" Dylan exclaimed, and they both raised their manicured hands in the air. "Yay!"

Noah's head was spinning. "Girls!" he yelled, and they quieted down immediately. "Fallon and I still need to discuss this." He didn't want her to take on such a huge obligation. He had another woman scheduled for an interview on Monday. This one came highly recommended from another partner in the office whose son no longer needed watching over.

"Why don't you two give me five more minutes under the fans? Then we can clean up. I'll talk to your dad and be right in to help."

They ran off and he let out a groan of relief. "They're like an army. I can't ask you to watch them all week while I work."

"You didn't ask. I offered. And I really want to. I love being with them, Noah. It's not a burden."

The offer was the answer to his problem and after seeing the three of them together today, he had no concerns about leaving his girls with Fallon. If anything, he was more worried they'd drive her crazy and away.

"They can be a handful," he warned her.

"And I can handle them however they behave. But I have a hunch they'd rather have me than someone new so they'll be on their best behavior."

He nodded. "Good point. I'm meeting with a promising candidate who can start whenever I'm ready so—"

"So talk to her, see how you feel, and if you like her, I can help the introduction with the girls. I've got this," she assured him.

His fingers itched to have her in his arms again, his hands in her silky hair, his lips on hers. Having her in his home was the next best thing.

"Do we have a deal?" she asked.

"We do. Now come seal it with a kiss."

And she did.

ON MONDAY, FALLON handled things at the gallery, listing the damaged items and turning the list over to the police. Worried about Clara, she checked on her boss by phone and though she offered to come by, the older woman insisted she just needed the break from work and to rest. She called the artists, explaining about the break-in and damage. The majority were understanding, though one or two had arrogance and ego in spades and took their anger out on Fallon. With one gentleman in particular, she'd had to threaten to hang up on him if he didn't moderate his tone and he'd backed down. Though he still said he was taking his commissions elsewhere. The day left her with a splitting headache, but the rest of the week Fallon spent with the girls.

She filled their time together with educational but fun activities. One day she took them to the Bronx Zoo, a delight for both girls, but mostly Dakota. The next day they visited Spyscape, an interactive museum the twins loved. On Thursday, they hit up The Paint Place, a studio that offered activities similar to the painting Fallon had done with the girls, but this one catered exclusively to kids and teens.

Fallon loved her days with the girls and evenings with Noah where the twins regaled him with stories of their day. She was beginning to like the family feeling too much considering she wasn't part of their lives that way. Come Monday, the girls would be the new nanny's responsibility. Noah had met and hired the woman at the beginning of the week. Her references were stellar and with some encouragement from Fallon, the girls had agreed to give Greta, a Swedish student here on a work visa, a real chance.

Too often, Fallon had to remind herself she was only Noah's girlfriend, not that they'd defined their status, but as two adults, she knew their relationship was monogamous. She just didn't know how long it would last and that meant not getting attached.

Though she knew better than to give her heart to the man and his children, she feared it was too late.

Chapter Seventeen

NOAH HAD TO admit the week Fallon watched the girls was the most productive one he'd had at work since the twins got off from school for the summer. Throughout the day, he'd receive messages from Fallon with pictures of the girls at their latest activity and he was astounded by the thought and effort she'd put into the babysitting offer. His favorite was a selfie of all three of his girls that he'd made his phone wallpaper so he could see it every time he picked up his cell.

His girls. The sentiment should have been a foreign one yet it felt right.

He arrived home Friday evening, planning to order in pizza and have them all watch a movie. He entered his apartment to find the entryway rug rolled up and the girls walking on coated paper, the soles of their feet covered in paint as they giggled and stepped to the beat of music Fallon had playing from her phone.

"Hello!" he called over the music.

"Daddy!"

"Nobody move!" Fallon ordered in a strict voice and to his surprise, they listened, halting in place.

"Hi. You're early," she said, her cheeks flushed as she met his gaze. "I planned to have this cleaned up by the time you got home."

He set his briefcase on the floor, far from the paint. "It's fine. Looks like you're having fun?"

"The best!" Dakota and Dylan exclaimed at the same time.

"Okay, girls. One at a time I'm carrying you to the tub. Who's first?"

He watched as she handled the twins like a pro, set them up in the shower, and returned to clean up, quickly and efficiently.

"Are you sure you've never been a full-time nanny?" he asked.

She laughed. "When you paint, you become meticulous about the mess and the cleanup process. Or at least I do. They promised not to step off the paper."

"Well, I'm impressed."

"Thanks."

"Stay for dinner and a movie?" he asked.

Swallowing, she shook her head. "I have plans."

He didn't like the pit that formed in his stomach at her words. "With?" he couldn't help but ask.

"My dad. I'm going there for dinner. It's been a while and my siblings and I have been taking turns subtly checking on him since his heart attack. He's the worst patient." She twisted her lips at the thought.

"Lizzie tries her best to take care of him," she said of the woman Fallon had told Noah her dad was dating. "But he's stubborn."

Relief filled him because she was seeing family. He'd never been jealous before and had a hard time with this particular emotion.

"How are you getting there?" he asked, knowing they lived outside the city.

She lifted one shoulder. "I'll Uber."

He nodded, glad she wasn't taking the subway at night.

"Thank you for this week," he said, not wanting her to feel like a babysitter when she was so much more. "I've never seen the girls so happy."

She smiled and it lit up her pretty eyes. "The week was a blast for me, too. They're so smart and fun to be around. Speaking of, I should check on them."

She turned and started in the direction of the girls' room and bathroom but Noah hooked an arm around her waist, stopping her from leaving.

He spun her around and clasped his hands on her waist. "If I didn't know better, I'd think you were trying to avoid me."

"Not at all," she assured him, running a hand over his chest and the shirt he'd unbuttoned on his way up the elevator. "I just need to work on my painting this weekend. I've been doing that when I go home at night but I had things at the gallery that are now destroyed. I'm refreshing my stock, so to speak." Then, as if to reassure him, she rose to her tiptoes and pressed a kiss to his lips.

"We're done!"

Fallon jumped back but he kept one arm around her waist. It was time the kids see this was more than friendship. He'd never brought a woman around them before and this was the first time they'd seen him kiss anyone.

He glanced at the twins to gauge their reaction. They'd showered and changed into pajamas, their hair wet and hanging around their shoulders.

"What's for dinner?" Dylan asked.

"I'm hungry!" Dakota said.

Neither mentioned finding him kissing Fallon. "Take the win," he said to Fallon, who was stiff in his arms.

Her muscles eased and she relaxed against him.

"We're ordering pizza and Fallon is going to have dinner with her father," he said.

After some moaning and groaning because she was leaving, Fallon said goodbye and he walked her to the door. "Everything good?" he asked her.

"I'm exhausted," she said, laughing.

"They can wear out an army. I might have freaked out when I found out Charlie was having twins but I admit now that starting and ending with two at once really is the easy way."

"Daddy! When's the food going to be here?" one of the girls called out.

She shook her head, an amused smile on her lips. "Go."

"Text me when you're home safe." He kissed her lips and she walked out the door.

INSTEAD OF GOING to her father's, Fallon called and told Lizzie she had a headache and wasn't up to the car ride to see them. Understanding as always, Lizzie told her to feel better. She promised to call her dad in the morning and walked home from Noah's, needing the fresh air and time to think, Noah's words about the twins playing around in her head.

Beginning and ending with two kids. In other words, he didn't want more children. She wasn't sure why she'd never thought about it before, especially considering how aware she'd been of their age difference. Fallon had always wanted a big family like she'd had growing up. Losing her mom had made her appreciate her brothers even more. No matter how overprotective they could be, she always considered herself lucky to have them.

Now she'd gone and fallen in love with a man who was finished with kids. Why not? He had the two most perfect girls in the world. They were already nine years old. Why would he want to start over with babies and diapers?

Blowing out a breath into the cold air, she raised her hand to grab a cab, suddenly overcome with the desire to be home faster. And when Brooke called, insisting she meet her for a drink, she agreed, needing a friend more than she wanted to be alone.

She redirected the cab driver to the small bar near her apartment where Brooke suggested they go. She paid, tipped, and hopped out, relieved Brooke was waiting at a small booth.

"Hi," she said, as she slid in across from her friend.

"Hi, yourself." Brooke had just come from work and was dressed in a black pencil skirt and pink blouse, her hair up in a loose bun. "I just got here. What do you want to drink?"

Fallon scanned through the drink menu, her gaze catching a delicious-looking frozen strawberry margarita.

"Yum!" Brooke said, eyes wide as she nodded. "Make it two of those!"

They waited for the server to approach and placed the order, then made small talk about life, then work, and Fallon filled Brooke in on the status at the gallery.

"The insurance company is coming next week to view the damage. After that, we can start the cleanup process."

"Does that mean you're on babysitting duty again next week?" Brooke asked.

Fallon shook her head. "No, actually…"

"Drinks, ladies," the server said, cutting off what Fallon had been about to say. He placed two margarita glasses filled with their drinks on the table.

Brooke lifted her drink and Fallon did the same. "To this friendship," she said with a smile.

"Hear, hear." They lightly tapped glasses and took their first sips of the delicious drink.

"So… back to my question. Are you still going to watch the twins next week?" Brooke asked.

Fallon felt the cool icy drink on her upper lip and caught the remainder with her tongue before replying. "That would be a no."

"Trouble in paradise?" Brooke asked.

"No, if anything things are too good and Noah said something today that has me wanting to pull away."

Brooke slid a finger over the top rim of her glass. "What could Mr. Perfect say to upset you so much? I can see it in your sad eyes." She braced her arms on the table, leaning close.

With a sigh, Fallon admitted the painful truth. "He

doesn't want more kids and… I think that's a deal-breaker for me."

"He said that? In those words?"

She shook her head. "He said when he found out Charlie, the girls' mom, was having twins he freaked out but he knows now that starting and ending with two really was the easy way. He implied it."

"Imply doesn't mean it's set in stone. Maybe you should talk to him?" Reaching out, Brooke put her hand over Fallon's. "I can see how hard you've fallen for him. You can't just walk away without a discussion. Even if it's about the hard things." She patted Fallon's hand and pulled hers back, taking another sip of her drink.

The thought of having that talk had Fallon freezing. "We haven't even had a relationship discussion. I'm not going to freak him out by mentioning kids so early!"

"The way I see things, you can stick it out and wait for the conversation to happen naturally or bring it up. What you shouldn't do is pull back because you're panicking."

She bit down on her lip. "I'll think about it," Fallon promised. But she honestly wasn't sure what she wanted to do.

Get in deeper and be hurt more once she confirmed the truth? Or bring up the baby discussion at this stage of their relationship and send Noah running anyway?

Either way, in the end there were two choices. End things with Noah and walk away from the best man she'd ever known, or give up on her personal dreams to accommodate his already set life. Her stomach hurt at the thought of either resolution.

"Fallon? Is that you?" She glanced up as Noah's brother, Liam, strode over to the table.

"Liam, hi!" She rose from her seat and accepted his hug. "It's good to see you. What are you doing in my neck of the woods?"

"I came with some friends." He tipped his head toward the bar. "But I have time for my brother's girl. Who's your friend?" he asked, his gaze on Brooke.

"Liam Powers, meet Brooklyn Snyder. Brooke, this is Noah's brother, Liam." She gestured between the two.

Eyes on Brooke, Liam lifted her hand and kissed the top. "A pleasure, Brooklyn."

Her friend's cheeks flushed red.

"Liam, you don't have to lay on the flirting so thick the second you meet her!"

"But she's beautiful."

Fallon rolled her eyes and Brooke laughed. "Oh, he's a charmer."

"See? She likes me. Mind if I join you ladies for a

few minutes," he said, rather than asked, and slid into the booth beside Fallon.

He gestured to the waiter and when the man stepped over, Liam ordered. "I'll have Macallan on the rocks. Refills?" he asked them.

"No, I'm still good," Brooke said.

"Same."

"So, Brooklyn, what do you do with your free time?"

"Oh my God!" Fallon threw up her hands, giving up on the flirt. Brooke could handle herself just fine.

Brooke laughed out loud. "I work at a financial firm and I don't have all that much time to spare," she lied. Brooke put in long hours at Fallon's dad's company but she was a valued employee who'd proven her worth. She could take time for herself. If she wanted to.

"I like you," Brooke said, still grinning. "But the truth is, I'm seeing someone."

Knowing better than to contradict or question her friend in front of the man she was letting down gently, Fallon focused on her drink and took a sip.

"Aah, she broke my heart." He placed a hand over the left side of his chest.

Fallon lightly nudged him in the ribs. "You really are a flirt." She hadn't seen that side of him when they were at his parents' house. He was lighter than Noah in personality, more initially friendly and easygoing. She'd liked both of Noah's brothers.

He shrugged. "A man's gotta take his shot. But that's my cue to go join my friends. Nice to meet you, Brooke. If you ever find yourself single, Fallon can get you my number." He winked, said his goodbyes, and strode away, every bit as cocky for having been shot down.

As soon as he was out of earshot, Brooke blew out a breath and fanned her face. "That man is potent."

Fallon studied her friend, confused by her conflicting behavior. "Then why turn him down?"

"Oh, I really am very busy at the office."

Fallon bit down on the inside of her cheek. "You know, if you ever want to talk about him, you can. It doesn't matter that he's my brother. You're my ride or die."

Brooke smiled but the sentiment didn't reach her eyes. "It's complicated and not worth digging into."

"Then consider going out with Liam… or any guy for that matter."

"I'll think about it," Brooke said lightly.

"Touché." Fallon lifted her drink and tipped it toward her friend. Because it wasn't lost on Fallon that Brooke had mimicked Fallon's own words about Noah right before Liam had shown up and interrupted them.

Brooke grinned and indulged in her drink.

EXHAUSTED AFTER PIZZA with the twins, a movie, and getting them to settle down and go to sleep, Noah slid between his sheets with a low groan.

Bracing a hand over his head, he leaned back and closed his eyes, his thoughts on Fallon. Though he appreciated her help with the girls, he wanted more time alone with her. He hated to ask his parents for yet more babysitting hours, though they loved being with their grandkids.

At times like this, he resented Charlie for her choices. He wasn't a single parent, had never planned on being one. When she was in New York, he'd given her all the time off she needed, especially when the girls were young. He loved them more than life but he was only human and needed alone time with the woman he… loved.

Jesus.

On the one hand, that felt like it had come out of nowhere, on the other, the emotion had been building from the moment he'd gotten rid of his attitude toward her and let her in. Gotten to know her. And convinced himself the age difference didn't matter, not if things between them were real. And they were, at least for him. With the time she gave to his girls and the way she looked at him, he believed she felt the same way.

His cell rang, distracting him, and he glanced at the screen, then swiped to open it and hit speaker. "Hey, Liam. How goes it?" he asked.

"It goes well. Spent the day at one of my investments and I'm happy to report they may be new but they're turning a profit." He sounded pleased and Noah was happy for him.

"That's great. You know how to pick 'em."

Both Noah's brothers were angel investors, working together to buy into companies, investing capital in a start-up in exchange for an equity stake in their business. It was their way of using their trust funds to give back to the community while building their portfolio and income at the same time.

"Anyway, guess who I ran into at a small bar near one of my investments?"

Noah sat up straighter in bed. "Who?"

"Your girlfriend, and she was with a gorgeous friend. Of course, I took my shot but she turned me down. Now tell me, aren't I a good-looking guy?"

Noah shook his head. His brother was such a ham. "You saw Fallon?" He thought she was with her father tonight. In fact, he was still waiting for her to text him she'd gotten home safely.

"Having drinks with her friend Brooklyn. Nice name, too."

He rolled his eyes. "Was she okay? I thought she was going to see her dad."

"Seemed fine to me. Anyway, just wanted to let you know I ran into her. Can you get away for a gym session this weekend?"

"I'm not sure but starting Monday I have a new nanny and the girls swore they'd be on their best behavior. Things should lighten up for me a little." More time to adjust his schedule and have things get back to normal. Greta had Saturdays free too and could set up playdates with the girls' friends. Once she survived one day with the twins, an invisible weight would lift from his shoulders.

"Sounds good. Let's talk then."

"Bye, Li."

"Bye."

Disconnecting the call, he leaned back in bed and debated calling Fallon. Ultimately, he decided to give her space, if that's what she needed. Hopefully she'd call or text before she went to sleep.

But when he woke up in the morning, he still hadn't heard from Fallon.

Chapter Eighteen

FALLON WOKE UP the next morning and immediately realized she hadn't checked in with Noah when she got home. He thought she'd gone to her dad's and had asked her to let him know she was home safe.

"Shit." Picking up her cell, she sent off a brief text apologizing, explaining she'd had a headache and was planning to go home but Brooke had called so she'd gone out with her instead, and had forgotten to call him when she got home.

After stopping in the bathroom, she pulled on her robe and walked into the kitchen and made herself a cup of much-needed caffeine. She and Brooke had ordered another drink and this one had been much heavier on the vodka. They'd ordered some fried appetizers but the food hadn't done much to soak up the alcohol. She had a slight headache this morning. Taking a long sip of coffee, she moaned at the rich flavor. Exactly what she needed.

She took a cup of Greek yogurt from the fridge and sat at her small table by the window overlooking the city and ate a light breakfast. Today was her first day to herself in a week and she debated what she wanted to do with it.

She'd spend some time painting, for sure, but first she wanted to visit with Clara. She wouldn't call first because she did not want to argue and end up being talked out of going over. Her day decided, she picked up her mug and empty yogurt cup and cleaned up.

She returned to the bathroom, brushed her teeth, and was about take a shower when the intercom app from the downstairs doorman buzzed on her phone. "Hello?"

"Ms. Sterling, you have a Mr. Powers here to visit."

"Oh!" What was Noah doing there? "Send him up, please." Tugging her robe tighter, she headed to the door to meet him.

Hearing the elevator ding in the hall, she cracked the door ajar, opening it when she heard his footsteps approach. "Noah! What are you doing here?"

"When I didn't hear from you last night, I was worried."

"I texted—"

"While I was already on my way over." He grasped her hand and led her inside.

"Why didn't you just call me?"

Once inside and the door closed, he took off his jacket, hanging it in the coat closet before spinning her around until her back was against the wall and he crowded in close. "Because I wanted to see you," he said and captured her mouth in a kiss.

Her lips parted in surprise and he was ready, sliding his tongue inside. She didn't know what had brought on this sudden visit but despite all the warnings in her head, she wasn't complaining. He was everything she wanted in a man, sexy, caring, and protective in the best way.

Kissing him back came naturally and soon things got more heated. She slid her hands beneath his hunter green T-shirt and together they pulled it over his head. He tossed it onto the floor and she splayed her hands over his warm, bare chest, her thumbs grazing his nipples.

With a groan, he slipped his hands between them and tugged on the sash of her robe, easily releasing the silk tie. She shrugged her shoulders and the robe fell from her shoulders and she lowered her arms so the garment slid to the floor.

She shivered and he covered her breasts with both hands, warming her body and arousing her with the touch of his palms. Dipping his head, he pressed long, slow kisses down her neck, along her collarbone until her knees trembled and desire consumed her.

"I need you," he said, undoing the button on his jeans and shoving them over his hips, snagging his boxer briefs as he pulled them down, then kicked them off.

Before she could blink he'd lifted her off the floor and she wrapped her legs around his waist, clasping her ankles at the small of his back just as he entered her with one smooth thrust.

He held her aloft with the strength of his body and the support of the wall behind her, his hips jerking upward with powerful drives she felt deep in her core. She locked her arms around his neck, looking into his hazel eyes, watching as they darkened, his jaw locked, and need filled his expression.

Every pump of his hips drove her higher, her own desire rising. One more shift of his lower body sent her soaring, her climax overtaking her.

"Noah!" She cried out his name, moaning through her explosive orgasm, which seemed to never end.

Three more thrusts and he slammed into her once more, stilling as he filled her over and over.

By the time he pulled out, her legs would not hold her and he scooped her into his arms, taking steady strides to the bathroom. He lowered her onto the closed toilet seat and she stared vacantly ahead, uncaring what came next, she felt so deliciously sated.

After turning on the shower, he lifted her into the stall and took over. He soaped her legs and thighs, working his way upward as he gently cleaned her, helping her wash and condition her hair, before he turned his attention to himself.

A little while later, she lay in bed, her head on his chest, her hair still damp. Neither cared. Silence took over and she was grateful. Her body still felt like Jell-O, but her breaths had finally smoothed out. So had her mind. She wasn't giving up this man unless and until she had to.

Don't go looking for trouble, her mother used to tell her, and she heard her mom's voice speaking to her now. The future loomed and it was scary, but it wasn't in her face yet. So, for the moment, she wasn't going anywhere.

Fallon spent the weekend with Noah. Somehow, he'd convinced his sister to give him twenty-four hours of free time and they made the most of it. Holed up in her apartment, ordering in food, and having sex. Lots and lots of amazing sex.

By the time he was ready to leave on Sunday morning, she was even more in love with the man. And she hoped the possible pain in the end was worth the beauty of now.

AFTER NOAH WENT home to the girls, Fallon dressed and headed to visit Clara. When she arrived, the doorman let her up and she stood knocking for a good five minutes before she grew worried and headed back downstairs, coming up to the concierge desk.

"Excuse me, but did you see Clara this morning?" she asked the doorman.

He shook his head. "No. Her son left a couple of hours ago but as far as I know, she's home. Why?"

"She's not answering and I'm worried. Do you have a spare key?"

"I'm not sure I should go in," he said, hesitating.

Fallon curled a hand into a frustrated fist at her side. "Clara hasn't been well and there's silence from inside. Please? I'll take full responsibility if she's upset with you. Please," she said again, more urgently this time.

He nodded. "Fine." He walked into the room behind him, shutting the door, then returned with a set of keys in his hand. "Let's go up."

Once outside the apartment door again, the doorman knocked hard, ringing the bell while Fallon shifted anxiously from foot to foot.

"I told you, nobody's answering. Open the door?"

He inserted the key in the lock, turned, and let them inside.

"Clara?" Fallon called out. She made her way through the apartment, checking the kitchen, the sitting room and then the family room, before walking into the bedroom where she found the older woman lying on the floor, unresponsive.

"Clara!" Fallon knelt down, picking up her weathered hand and feeling for a pulse. Finding one, she yelled, "Call 911!" to the doorman who'd waited at the entrance to the apartment.

"Clara?" Fallon asked in a soothing voice. She spoke to her in low tones for what felt like forever until the paramedics finally arrived.

She stepped back to let the professionals do their job and when they told her what hospital they'd be taking Clara to, Fallon rushed downstairs to hail a taxi.

Hours passed as Fallon paced the floor in the hospital waiting room. She'd told the paramedics about Clara's heart condition but beyond that she felt useless. Not only that, she had visions of the night her mom died, nobody letting her into the room, the explanation given by her dad, that someone had hurt her mommy and she was in heaven now. And that overwhelming feeling and pit of pain, anguish, and fear.

She glanced around at the sterile, beige walls and down at the empty table in the center of the room. There were no magazines to read, not that she could concentrate, nobody to talk to, and by the time noon passed, she was scared and lonely. She wanted someone to keep her company but she *needed* Noah. She knew he had the girls to care for but she couldn't stop herself from picking up her phone and dialing his number.

He arrived not long after and she rushed to him, allowing him to wrap her in his comforting arms.

"Any news?" he asked.

She stepped back and shook her head. "Not a word."

Together they sat back down to wait but she felt better with Noah by her side. She wasn't up to explaining the feelings that this experience brought back, feeling if she talked about her mom, she'd cry and not stop.

"I can stay until early evening. Then I need to go home to the girls so Shannon can leave," he said, regret in his tone as she threaded his fingers through hers.

"I'm just grateful you came."

"Family of Mrs. Clara Morganville?" A female nurse stepped into the room and glanced around.

Finally. She popped up from her seat and Noah rose, standing beside her. "That's me." Fallon raised a hand uselessly.

"And you're her…?"

"Daughter," she automatically said, knowing if she didn't claim a familial relationship not only wouldn't they give her information but they wouldn't allow her to see Clara.

"Your mother is stable."

"Oh, thank God." For the first time since finding Clara on the floor, Fallon's heartbeat began to slow to a normal rate. This wasn't a repeat of the past. Clara was okay. "Can I see her?"

The other woman nodded. "Of course. But she's asleep. You can check on her now and come back tomorrow. Follow me."

"Was it her heart?" she asked.

"The doctor ran tests. We should have the results in a few hours."

Noah clasped her hand. "I need to get back to the girls. You're okay now that you have news?"

She looked at him, seeing in his taut expression that he was upset by the need to leave her.

"I'm good. Promise." She rose to her tiptoes and kissed his cheek. "Thank you for coming. I appreciate it so much."

He nodded. "I'd stay but—"

"You're needed at home. Go." She squeezed his hand. "I'm fine."

After saying goodbye to Noah, Fallon sat by Clara's bedside. Her skin was pale and paper-thin but her breathing was steady and that's all Fallon cared about for now. She stayed until the nurse returned and encouraged her to go home and return tomorrow, when hopefully Clara would be more alert.

Worried but relieved at the prognosis, Fallon agreed.

But Clara's scare had her taking the first LIRR train to Old Brookville to visit her father. Canceling last night had been one thing but she'd seen firsthand how quickly a person's health could turn and she wanted to see her dad in person and make sure he was okay.

She showed up without calling first and knocked on the front door.

Lizzie greeted her, her eyes wide with surprise. "Fallon! I wasn't expecting you today."

Stepping into the house, Fallon pulled the woman into a hug she desperately needed, inhaling her familiar scent that said family to Fallon. Once they'd moved into this home after her mom died, Lizzie had become like a second mother to her and Brooklyn like a sister. She'd listened to Fallon's teenage angst and dried her tears.

"I'm sorry I canceled last night," Fallon said, feeling suddenly emotional. A lump rose to her throat and stayed there.

"Honey, you're allowed. What's going on?" Lizzie ushered her inside and took her jacket, hanging it in the hall closet.

"Is Dad home?"

"He's napping in the study but come into the

kitchen. Let me make you a cup of tea and we can talk until he wakes up."

She nodded and swiped at her eyes. "Sorry. I'm all verklempt." She laughed as she used the Yiddish word for emotional that Lizzie had taught her growing up. Lizzie and Brooklyn were Jewish and she'd learned many fun words with Brooke's mom around.

"I see that and I want to know why."

Once in the kitchen, Fallon sat on a barstool and let Lizzie bustle around the large room with state-of-the-art stainless appliances and granite countertops. Her father had said the kitchen was old and needed a remodel but Fallon suspected he was giving Lizzie a place to make her own inside the main house. No doubt her father wanted Lizzie to give up the guesthouse and move in but nobody had mentioned it out loud. Yet.

Lizzie made two cups of tea and placed their vanilla chamomile drink on the counter, followed by milk and sugar, knowing Fallon liked her drink sweet. Though tea was a trigger, with Lizzie she found it soothing, as having Lizzie around lessened the pain of her mother's passing in some small way. "So. What has you so worked up?" Lizzie asked.

Fallon drew a deep breath and explained what had happened with Clara this morning. "Seeing her lying on the floor, I thought she was dead. And while I waited to hear something in the hospital, I had all these memories of the night Mom died. It was awful."

"Oh, honey." Lizzie placed a hand over Fallon's briefly. "But she's okay? Your boss?"

Nodding, Fallon forced herself to take a steadying breath. "She is. I still don't know exactly what happened. Her son should have been with her and wasn't. She's been so sick lately. Now they'll find out what's wrong." And hopefully put her on the road to recovery.

She made her tea the way she liked it, adding a healthy drop of milk and two sugars, then took a sip and sighed. "So good. Reminds me of the times you'd make us this same tea when Brooke or I were upset."

Lizzie smiled. "So much teenage drama with you two."

They both laughed.

"How's Dad?" Fallon asked. "When I left the hospital, all I wanted to do was come see him for myself."

"Oh, Alexander is well behaved at home. It's the office where I worry. But he looks well. He's still working too many hours despite Aiden and Jared being there to shoulder the workload." She lifted her shoulder. "But he wouldn't be the Alexander we know if he wasn't trying to do more and act like he's still a thirty-year-old man." She shook her head, then lifted her teacup and took a sip.

"Anything else? You still seem so... heavy hearted."

"Nothing I want to talk about. Brooke and I had a good heart-to-heart last night. I ended up having a drink with her before I went home. And she gave me some good advice. I just need time to figure some things out."

Lizzie nodded. "You have a good head on your shoulders. You'll do what's best."

"Well, this is a nice surprise!"

At the sound of her father's voice, Fallon turned. He stood in the entry to the kitchen and she jumped up and hugged him tight. "Hey, Dad."

"Hey, princess. Are you feeling better?"

She nodded, not wanting to give him anything to worry about. "I just wasn't up to the trip yesterday. But I'm here now. How are *you* feeling?" He looked a little tired, definitely thinner, though that was what the doctor ordered. Better eating, better health.

"I'm good. Don't worry about your old man," he said.

Laughing, she hit his shoulder. "Don't call my dad old!"

She spent the rest of the evening with her family, soaking up the goodness and being grateful for what she did have. A call to the hospital told her Clara was improving. And though part of her still thought pulling back from Noah was the smart thing to do, he'd been so kind, rushing out and leaving the girls with his sister to come sit with her at the hospital, she couldn't do it. Nor did she want to.

So she texted him and let him know where she was and that she might sleep here and go straight to the hospital to visit Clara in the morning. In the afternoon, she thought maybe she'd stop by the closed gallery and do some painting. She'd been working on two special pieces there, one for each of the twins, recreating what they'd each liked about the original canvas that had been destroyed.

Fallon might be good at painting but she was the worst at protecting her heart.

Chapter Nineteen

"CLARA! YOU'RE AWAKE," Fallon said, as she walked into the hospital room and found her boss and mentor sitting up and alert. "I brought you your favorite blend of tea." She held the large cannister in her hands. "I didn't think flowers that would make your allergies go crazy were a good idea. And I'm sure they're monitoring your food. So… tea."

"Thank you! I was running out at home. Don't tell Oliver but I really prefer my own blend to his special tea. But enough about that. I understand you found me? I don't know what would have happened if you hadn't come by." She held out her hand for her to clasp.

She put the tea on the moveable tray and took the older woman's fragile hand in hers. "Clara, I adore you. I'm just glad you're going to be okay. Was it your heart?"

"No, actually. The tests came back the same as last time I had a checkup. My own cardiologist stopped by. But they're rerunning blood tests. There was an abnormality or something and they want to retest to be sure. I didn't pay much attention. I do know they're giving me saline and flushing out my system. They want me to stay a few days but I'm just glad I'm finally feeling better."

"Good. Make sure you follow the doctor's orders. Has anyone contacted Oliver?" Or maybe the doorman told him about his mother's collapse and to what hospital she'd been taken.

"No. I haven't heard from him. When I sat up and was dizzy, I tried calling for him but he didn't answer. And I passed out before I could get to my phone."

"Well, you're on the road to recovery and that's what matters. Oliver will turn up." He always does, she thought, but didn't say as much out loud.

They sat and talked about the work that had been done in the gallery. "The insurance company promised to cut the check soon and as you know, I had workers in last week. You can see it today if you'd like to stop by," Clara said.

Fallon nodded. "In the meantime, when I leave here I'll call Sylvie and tell her we can open tomorrow!" Excitement fluttered in her belly at the thought. "I missed the place while we were gone."

A knock sounded on the door. "Time to take your vitals, Mrs. Morganville," a young nurse said.

"That's my cue. You should nap when she's finished." Fallon bent over and kissed her cheek. "Take care and I'll talk to you soon."

She left the hospital and took an Uber to the gallery, unlocking the door and letting herself in. Since she wasn't ready for customers, she locked the door, flipped on the lights, and walked through the gallery, pleased with the changes. Clara had obviously taken the opportunity to have the entire gallery side painted and new sconces put in over where the artwork would hang. For someone who'd been laid up in bed, she sure had been working behind the scenes or her decorator friend had. Either way, Fallon was in love with the new look.

Tomorrow she'd get started on checking in with their usual artists but today, she had some painting of her own to do. She set up at her favorite easel, turned music on loud on her cell phone, and settled in to paint for the girls.

As usual when she worked, she got lost in the color mixes, choices, and strokes. By the time she looked up and glanced at the clock on her phone, hours had passed and she had messages from Brooke, her brother, Remy, who she hadn't spoken to in too long, and Dex's wife, Samantha, who wanted to make lunch plans and catch up.

She spent a few minutes rinsing the brushes off in the back and setting them out to dry before walking back into the room. Something smelled off and she sniffed, then sniffed again.

She smelled smoke.

A glance at the door to the gallery, a door she knew she'd left open, was now shut and she rushed over and turned the knob. To her relief, it hadn't self-locked and she flung it open only to see the room filling with smoke.

Slamming the door closed because the paints and removers in *this* room were flammable, she grabbed her bag and jacket and ran to the front door. She unlocked it and tried to push but it wouldn't budge. Using her body weight, she flung her shoulder against the door to no avail.

She wasn't panicked... yet. The smoke had begun to seep under the small door to the gallery but she was still safe in here. She looked outside and had trouble seeing why the exit was jammed but it felt like something heavy was blocking the door and preventing it from moving. And the emergency exit in the back was on the gallery side.

One thing she knew: she had to get out of here.

Grabbing her phone, she dialed 911 and reported the fire, and the fact that she was locked inside the gallery. Then she called Noah because his apartment was close by. He answered on the first ring and she quickly explained her situation.

The fire alarm went off at a deafening level while she continued to do everything she could to move the door but it was jammed tight. Soon, her shoulder couldn't take the pain of hitting against the glass. Giving up, she grabbed a towel and wrapped it over her nose and mouth, then lowered herself to the floor near the entrance and settled in to wait for help, praying it got here before the fire broke through the wall.

"LET'S GO, GIRLS! Katy's mom is going to be here any minute to pick you up," Noah called out. He'd been waiting for them for ten minutes, knowing to start early. God help him when they became teenagers.

A little while later, he'd had them put their jackets on and took them downstairs where their friend and her mom waited to take the girls to the movies. They'd asked if they could have their friend over and when he'd called, Jan, Katy's mom, asked if she could bring them to the theater. He'd planned to spend the day in the office while the girls hung out with their friend but he was happy to hand them off for a few hours.

He returned upstairs to get himself together and then he planned on going to the hospital where Fallon said she'd be visiting with Clara. He'd felt guilty leaving her yesterday, the only thing making him feel better had been the fact that Clara was stable. At least he hadn't left Fallon distraught and worried.

Once upstairs he took a quick shower and dressed, then grabbed his car keys just as his phone alerted him to a call and he saw Charlie's photo on the screen.

He answered her FaceTime call, hoping he could get her off quickly since the girls weren't here. He was eager to see Fallon.

He swiped to accept the call. "Charlie, hey!"

"Hi, Noah. How are you?"

"Everything's good. You just missed the girls, though. They went to the movies with Katy and her mom."

"What did they go see?" she asked, obviously eager for even the smallest detail about her girls.

He told her and she sighed. "I really wanted to take them to see it next time I'm home."

"I'm sure you can catch it on streaming with them. You know they love to watch the same thing over and over."

She nodded, tucking her dark brown hair behind her ear. "How is... Fallon's her name, right? The twins said she watched them last week and the new nanny is starting tomorrow."

At Fallon's name, he stiffened but nodded. "Listen, she's good with them. Took them to educational fun things every day. I trust her and if I trust her, then you should too." He hoped that would stave off any argument over last week's babysitting arrangement.

"Relax, I'm not going to give you a hard time. Of course I trust your judgment. I just wanted to say I'm happy for you. Even a little jealous of the time she's spending with the kids." Charlie let out a nervous laugh at the admission.

"There's nothing wrong with you following your dreams. And I understand how much you miss the girls. I would too. But I can promise you, Fallon is not trying to replace you in their eyes. She just genuinely likes spending time with them. They're fun to be around… when they're behaving." He chuckled.

"Actually, that's part of why I'm calling. I'm coming home for a long weekend. I really miss the kids." Tears shimmered in her eyes and he nodded in understanding.

"Just email me the dates and I'll clear our schedules so you have all the time you want with them," he promised.

"Thank you. Can they come sleep at the hotel with me?"

"Of course."

She let out a relieved breath. "You're a good man, Noah. Giving me this opportunity and not holding it against me."

"I may not have followed any dreams but I can understand having a passion for something. I watch

Dakota and she's so much like you. Curious to learn and find out about everything. Go back to your dig and relax. Your girls love you. I'll see you soon."

She smiled, her mood obviously lighter, and said goodbye. When he cleared the screen, he saw he'd gotten a message from Fallon. She'd gone to the gallery for the day so instead of a trip to the hospital, he settled into his office to work.

No sooner had he cracked open a brief when his phone rang again. This time he was pleased with the incoming call.

He swiped the screen. "Fallon, hi!"

"Noah, quick. I'm trapped in the gallery, on the painting side. Something's blocking the front exit. I can't get out and there's a fire next door. I called 911 but if you're home, you're so much closer."

"I'm home and I'm coming." He was out of his seat and running, phone still in his hand. "Stay calm and try not to panic. Wait by the door and I'll be there soon." Grabbing his keys, he slipped into his shoes and rushed down to his car.

No way a car would get him there quickly so he decided to run. Sheer adrenaline and fear drove him. He didn't know what he'd do if anything happened to the woman he loved. She'd become such an intertwined, important part of his life, he couldn't imagine not having her as part of his world.

He arrived to see two heavy cement blocks, one on top of the other, obstructing the door to the art studio side of the gallery. No wonder she couldn't make it budge.

Inside, Fallon sat on the floor, one arm wrapped around her knees, a towel over her nose and mouth.

Sirens sounded in the distance as he attempted to lift the first block but it wouldn't move. He braced his legs and pushed and the block fell over to the other side.

One down.

Sirens sounded in the distance but he smelled the smoke and wasn't wasting time. He assumed the same position and lifted the second block enough to roll it to the other side.

By now, Fallon was aware of his presence and the moment he removed the obstacles, she pushed open the door, stepped outside, and flung herself into his arms, sobbing.

"Shh. I've got you." He hugged her tight, ignoring the smell of smoke clinging to her clothes until finally she stepped out of his embrace, still breathing heavily.

"Oh my God, Noah, thank you!" Tears streamed down her face, and her hair was wild and falling over her shoulders. "I couldn't move it and the alarm was going off, the smoke got heavy on my side and…"

"It's okay." He brushed her hair off her face and

looked into her eyes. "You're okay."

But he might never be the same, the panic he felt running here and the fear lodged in his chest felt like it would never go away. He couldn't show her his terror if he wanted to calm her down.

"Come on. Let's move away from here to where it's safer." He led her a short distance away, hoping the firemen got here soon.

"The whole time I sat there, I kept thinking, who would want to destroy the gallery?"

"It couldn't be faulty wiring?" he asked.

She shook her head. "It's unlikely. Clara is meticulous about the building being up to code. She owns the property. And she adores the gallery. First the vandalism, now a fire?" She turned toward the building that now had smoke billowing from the top.

"Okay, so who stands to gain?"

"The only person who would benefit from insurance money is Clara and the gallery is her baby." As she spoke, her eyes opened wide.

"*Her baby,*" Noah said, reading her mind. "Her son."

"Oliver. He's been missing lately. Never around when he should be. He hasn't been to the hospital to visit his mother. She hasn't even heard from him."

Before he could reply, a fire truck pulled to a stop in front of the building.

A man jumped out of the front cab and they rushed over to him, ignoring the small crowd that had gathered.

"What happened?" he asked.

Fallon explained how she'd been painting on one side and the fire started on the other. How she'd been deliberately barricaded inside. "There are flammable liquids inside," she informed him.

With a nod, he rushed off to talk to his men. Another fireman strode over and instructed them to clear the area and they crossed the street, waiting and watching with the other onlookers.

The paramedics and the police arrived shortly after. Though Fallon hadn't been out of breath nor had she exhibited any worrying signs of smoke inhalation, the medical team had insisted on checking her out.

Once she'd been cleared, she'd given her statement to the police and fire investigator on scene, also mentioning what she knew of Oliver's behavior. They'd both taken notes and said they'd be in touch if they had more questions.

Noah and Fallon walked back to his apartment, his arm around her shoulders.

"I didn't outright accuse Oliver," she said. "I just pointed out his suspicious behavior, his constant need for money, and how he wasn't a fan of the gallery. But I hope the police rule him out. For Clara's sake," she murmured.

"So do I." But Noah's gut told him the other man had a lot to answer for before that could happen.

Chapter Twenty

O NCE NOAH AND Fallon got back to the apartment she was free to talk and react to the traumatizing events of earlier since the twins weren't there. If Noah hadn't gotten there when he had... She'd begun to hear the crackling of flames next door. God, she'd been so frightened and she'd had to sit by uselessly as smoke and fire threatened from next door.

Tears formed in her eyes as she realized the gallery had been destroyed. It would take a long time to rebuild, she thought sadly.

She wrapped her hands around a cup of hot tea, taking comfort from the steaming mug and familiar chamomile smell. When Noah asked what he could get for her, she'd wanted the drink that reminded her of her mother. Instead of running from that pain, she'd needed to feel close to her. Besides, coffee wouldn't calm her down and she needed to get rid of the panic that still clawed inside her.

Noah sat by her side, leaving her alone with her thoughts, and she was grateful for the comfortable silence. She'd already let her family know what happened and that she was fine, wanting them to hear the news about the gallery from her and not on the news.

She'd left her phone and bag behind, and hoped they'd be salvageable when the fire department was finished. Noah's phone rang, startling her out of her thoughts.

"Hello?" he said, taking the call.

"Yes, she's here. Hold on." He covered the phone with his hand. "It's one of the police officers you spoke to at the scene." They'd given him Noah's number to reach her if they had further questions. "Are you up to it?"

She nodded and took the phone. "Hello? This is Fallon Sterling."

"Ms. Sterling, this is Officer Jones, we met at the fire site earlier. I'm at the hospital where Mrs. Clara Morganville is being treated. I came to inform her of the situation at her gallery and she's been sedated."

"Why?" she asked, stiffening. "What's wrong?"

"Apparently there was an incident earlier we think is related to the fire. Do you think you could come down here to answer some questions since Ms. Morganville can't at the moment?"

"Yes. I'll be over soon." She disconnected the call and met Noah's curious gaze. "Something happened at the hospital. They had to sedate Clara and the police want to ask me some questions."

He raised an eyebrow. "Do you need a lawyer?" he

asked, his protective instincts obviously kicking in.

She shook her head. "I think he just wants answers he can't get from Clara until she's awake."

"I'll take you. Are you ready?"

She nodded and they left for the hospital where they received the shock of their lives.

Sitting alone with Officer Jones in the waiting room, the door closed, he explained how when he'd come to question Clara—Fallon had informed him earlier the gallery owner was in the hospital—he'd walked in on officers from another precinct arresting her son, Oliver.

"Why?" Fallon asked. "And why is Clara sedated? She was doing well when I visited yesterday." Noah clasped her hand in his and squeezed for reassurance.

The office looked at her as he spoke. "It seems he was caught in the act of attempting to smother his mother with a pillow. An orderly held him down until the police arrived."

"What?!" she cried, jumping up from her seat. "I don't understand."

"Luckily for us, he was in an angry, frustrated, and talkative mood after the police arrived and cuffed him. It seems Mr. Morganville is in debt to some very dangerous people."

"That doesn't surprise me," she said as she lowered herself back into her chair. "Oliver always needed money from his mother."

The officer nodded. "According to the tests run by the hospital, she was being slowly poisoned, which is why you found her collapsed in her apartment."

"Oh my God." Fallon covered her mouth with her hand.

"Mr. Morganville was counting on killing his mother for the insurance money on the gallery. He figured they'd label her cause of death old age or a heart attack and leave it at that. But she lived, thanks to you. And then he heard Mrs. Morganville tell you she was leaving the business to you, cutting him out of the lucrative real estate and gallery."

She nodded. "She just told me recently and I was shocked. But—"

He held up a hand, indicating he wanted to continue. "When Mr. Morganville discovered you were an obstacle to his inheritance, he decided to get rid of you, too."

Noah stiffened in his seat and she grabbed his hand.

"He watched you and waited until you were alone in the gallery, then set the fire in the other side, assuming you were too busy with your painting to notice until it was too late. And to make sure, he set the cement blocks by the front door, locking you inside."

Oliver had attempted to murder her and Fallon was too stunned to speak.

"And Clara?" Noah asked.

"Was overwrought and they sedated her to keep her calm." He went on to ask more questions about Oliver and his relationship with his mother and what Fallon knew about why he needed the money.

"He's in custody?" Noah asked, obviously wanting confirmation.

"Yes. And with two attempted murder charges, both premediated, I don't see him making bail. Not that he seems to have the money to pay it even if he did."

"Good," she said. "Good." She rubbed her forearms with her hands, chilled from all the revelations.

The officer informed Fallon he'd call if he had more questions, then left them alone in the room.

She turned to Noah. "That was… a lot."

"Your instincts about him were spot-on," he said.

"I didn't have murder on my bingo card." She tried to make a joke of things but it fell flat, even to her.

Noah merely pulled her onto his lap and held her tight, neither of them saying another word.

FALLON COULDN'T SEE Clara until the next day but

she was waiting when the hospital opened the doors to visitors. She walked into Clara's room.

Her friend, boss, and mentor lay in the bed, facing the window overlooking the parking lot.

"Clara?" Fallon said softly.

She turned, sadness etched into the grooves of her face. "Fallon, I'm so glad you're here."

"I came yesterday but they'd given you something to help you sleep."

Clara gestured to the lone chair in the room. "Come sit."

Fallon pulled the chair closer to the bed and lowered herself into it. "I've been so worried about you. I'm so glad to see you awake."

"I'm fine now... or getting there. I'm still a little weak when I walk and need the cane. But I'm hoping the side effects will minimize over time."

Fallon nodded. Silence fell and she wasn't sure what to say or how to broach the subject of Oliver or Clara's emotional state given what had transpired yesterday.

"Go ahead. Ask me. I see the wheels turning in your brain."

"I just wanted to say I'm sorry about Oliver. How are you handling things?" She placed a hand over Clara's. "And is there anything I can do for you?"

Clara treated her to an obviously forced smile. "I

thought I knew my son. I understood he was arrogant, pompous, and entitled. In no world did I think he'd try to kill me, his mother, or you." Turning her hand over, she squeezed Fallon's.

"You know about the fire then?" Fallon hadn't been sure how she was going to tell her.

"The police came by to ask me more questions and they told me. I'm so sorry."

"Don't apologize for something Oliver did. You aren't responsible."

Clara sighed. "It's hard not to feel as though I failed as a parent."

Although Fallon understood, Clara didn't need the emotional baggage that kind of guilt would bring. "He's a grown man who makes his own decisions."

"And the gallery." She blinked back tears. "I can't believe he thought by getting rid of us both he'd have the money he owed some dangerous people."

"You'll be okay. I know I'm not your biological daughter but you'll always have me."

Clara's eyes filled with tears and she reached for a tissue on the moveable tray by her bed and dabbed at her eyes. "I'm so grateful for you."

"Same here," Fallon whispered, a lump lodged in her throat.

"And don't worry about me. I didn't make it to this age without being tough. I'll survive my son's betrayal and come out stronger. And we will rebuild the gallery. I promise."

Fallon managed a bob of her head. She was as overcome as Clara with their conversation. But she promised herself whatever big family events she had, Clara would be a part of them.

Chapter Twenty-One

O NE WEEK HAD passed since the fire. Without the gallery to go to, Fallon was at loose ends. She spent her days with Clara, first at the hospital, making sure she was emotionally okay after the trauma with Oliver, and then helping her get home and settled in. The older woman had grown stronger after the toxins had been flushed from her body, and she resisted laying around in bed.

Her son was in jail. Clara, for as much as she loved her child, refused to visit him or support him by paying for an attorney. Fallon couldn't imagine the pain her friend was feeling but she was there for her, helping her through it.

The twins' mother had come for a visit and she'd taken over time with the girls. The new nanny even had time off her first week on the job. Charlie had brought the girls to her hotel, giving Fallon and Noah plenty of nighttime togetherness. There were some nights he had dinner with his kids and Charlie but most times, he was with Fallon and she soaked up his singular attention.

Fallon hadn't yet met Charlie but today was Liam's

birthday and she would see her at Noah's parents' house for a family get-together. To say she was antsy would be an understatement.

For whatever reason, she had this vision of Charlie as a worldly woman who would judge Fallon for her youth and relationship with Noah. But she was the twins' mother and Fallon intended to do her best to win her over.

The girls were with their mother, so Noah picked up Fallon at her apartment and they drove to Westchester County. The ride took about forty minutes and Fallon looked out the window at the green leaves on the trees.

Noah placed a hand on her thigh, stilling the tapping movement she hadn't been aware of doing. "Are you nervous?" he asked.

"A little. I just want Charlie to like me. She's the twins' mom and she means so much to them."

"Hey. She's as easygoing as you are. Don't worry about it. So, tell me what you bought Liam for his birthday. No pressure or anything but you have a reputation to live up to."

She let out a laugh. "Oh, I think I did a good job. You'll have to wait and see."

He squeezed her knee and she shrieked in surprise. "Ow! What was that for?"

"I can't believe you won't tell me first."

"Fine, Mr. Impatient. I bought him a set of candles. They're called Connoisseur Candles for Men. They smell like different smells a guy would like. Whisky, gin, tobacco, and bourbon. Happy now?"

He laughed. "Perfect. You're good at gift giving."

"Thank you. Just wait until the girls see their birthday presents."

That was another thing she'd devoted time to this week. Working on her painting. She had two special canvases, one for Dakota and one for Dylan, their names worked into the design, in the hot pink and purple colors they'd loved on the original work. Their birthday was next month and she couldn't wait.

He'd managed to distract her with conversation and soon they'd pulled into the driveway of his parents' home. A rental car was already parked there, as were a couple of other vehicles. Apparently, they weren't the first ones to arrive.

They walked into the house, the noise coming from the large kitchen where everyone had gathered. She put her gift on a table, as did Noah, and they went to greet the family.

Liam met her gaze first, a charming smile on his handsome face. Simon nodded at her in greeting. He was more serious than Liam, less so than Noah. Fallon might prefer Noah's fuller features but there was no doubt the brothers were a good-looking trio.

She lifted her hand as a hello and left Noah with his siblings as she stopped to talk to his mother who was as warm and welcoming as the first time Fallon had met her.

"Daddy! Fallon!" The twins came running into the room, their excitement tangible, no doubt because they'd been with their mom for most of the week.

"Hi, girls!"

"Guess where we went? To the place where we learned all about dinosaurs. There was a trampoline and we tried to jump as high as the tallest dino. And there was a dig site just like where Mom works! And a drawing part where we made our own dinosaur pictures!" Dakota exclaimed, finally seeming to run out of breath.

Dylan was calmer than her sister.

"That sounds amazing!" Fallon smiled at both girls.

"They definitely had fun," a pretty woman with shoulder-length dark hair said. "I'm Charlie," the girls' mother said.

Considering the twins had mixed them up from behind, she must have gotten it cut recently and the shape accentuated her attractive features.

"Hi. I'm Fallon. But you know that already." She met the other woman's gaze and there was no doubt she was sizing Fallon up the same way Fallon had just done to her.

Dylan and Dakota drifted toward the counter with their grandmother's chocolate chip cookies just waiting for them, leaving Fallon alone with Charlie.

"I've heard so much about you," she said. "The girls can't stop raving about all the adventures they had with you while you watched them for Noah." She sounded warm and sincere, and the butterflies in Fallon's stomach receded a bit.

"I tried to keep things fun and educational. They're wonderful girls."

"Thank you. I miss them so much. But I committed to the length of the excavation and I really am loving it."

Fallon understood being torn. "If it's any consolation, the girls seem enthralled with what you're doing. Well, mostly Dakota, but they talk about your job with awe and pride."

Charlie tipped her head and her expression softened. "That's so nice of you to say. Mom guilt. It's a bitch," she said, laughing. "So, they tell me you paint?"

"Is everything okay here?" Noah drew up beside them, joining the conversation, and not-so-discreetly slipping a protective arm around Fallon's shoulders.

"Go away, Noah. We're getting to know each other," Charlie said lightly.

Fallon chuckled. "She's right. Everything is fine."

"I'm glad. I want you two to like one another."

"No worries there," Charlie said. "I can tell how much Fallon cares about the girls. That's what matters to me. Plus, you're nice." Charlie winked.

Fallon grinned, liking how she read Noah and wasn't afraid to let him know what she was thinking. No wonder they were such good co-parents.

Noah picked a pretzel from a bowl on the counter and took a bite. "Then I suppose I'm not needed here."

"Exactly what I said when you walked over. I'm not going to bite. And, for what it's worth, I approve, not that you need that from me."

Fallon released a breath she hadn't been aware of holding. "We may not need it but I respect you as the twins' mom too much not to care. So thank you. That means a lot."

Noah pressed a kiss to Fallon's cheek. "Anyone want a soda? Water?"

Both Fallon and Charlie gave him their preference, Diet Coke for Charlie and club soda for Fallon, and he strode away to play bartender.

The rest of the day passed with the same flow and dynamic, Fallon feeling comfortable with his family, and for that she was grateful. The twins conned her and Charlie into playing a game of Twister in the family room, which they did. With an audience.

They ate burgers and hot dogs, Liam's choice for his birthday lunch, like a kid, and after they finished, Nina asked Noah to help her reach something in the hall closet which she used as a pantry. And Fallon found herself talking to Simon about how he and Liam became angel investors.

All in all, she'd call the day a success.

NOAH'S MOTHER NEEDED him to pull a package of paper towels from the top shelf of the closet, so he followed her into the hallway and grabbed the bundle, handing it to her.

"There you go. This has been a great day, Mom. Thanks for making it so easy to have Charlie and Fallon." His parents liked Charlie but she wasn't always included in his family gatherings. Because she was here for such a short time, he'd wanted to give her as much time with the girls as he could.

"Of course, honey."

Turning so he could return to the family room, he stopped when his mother called his name.

He pivoted back around to find a concerned look on her face. "Mom? Is everything okay?"

She nodded but he got the sense she wasn't being one hundred percent truthful. He knew his mother, she wanted to have her say and all he could do was wait her out.

"You're right. Today was fun. Liam is so antsy to open his presents. He's such a kid sometimes," she said with a loving smile.

Noah chuckled. "He definitely is."

"And Fallon is good with the girls. That was a mean game of Twister they played."

Yeah. With her body bent over, her ass out, his dick grew hard and he'd been tempted to walk up behind her and pull her against him to relieve the ache.

"Fallon's a lovely young woman," his mother said, bringing his mind out of the gutter. Not the thing to be thinking about with his mom right here.

Noah nodded. "I agree. I'm glad you like her."

"But—"

He narrowed his gaze, his defenses rising. "But what?" he asked, unable to control the bite in his tone. The last thing he wanted was to listen to any complaints about the woman who was perfect for him.

"Isn't she a little young for you?"

And there it was. The elephant in the room the times Fallon had been with his family. He'd come to terms with the fact. And that's all it was. A fact. Numbers. They had too much in common for him to let perception get in the way of *them*. He didn't need anyone getting in the middle of his feelings for Fallon

Just One More Temptation

or bringing up potential pitfalls.

"Can you keep your concerns to yourself?" He moderated his tone because he knew his mother meant well and he didn't want to hurt her feelings.

His mom reached out and touched his cheek in a move he knew all too well. "I'm just worried about you. A young girl like that? She loves your kids. There's no doubt she'll want a baby one day and I know you've said you're finished after the twins. How do you plan to deal with that once you're in so deep both of you risk getting hurt?" she asked.

Once he was in deep? He was already there. The possibility of losing Fallon made his stomach twist in pain. He rubbed a hand over his face and groaned.

Happy bubble burst, he thought, wishing he could glare at his mother, but she had a point. "How about you not borrow trouble?"

Except she'd tossed a grenade in his lap and now it was all he could think about. His fingers curled into fists at his sides, frustration running through him.

"Okay." She held up both hands. "I just had to say my piece."

"Thank you for caring." It was the best he could manage to say and still keep things peaceful between them.

She nodded, then turned and walked back to the family room, leaving him to mull over her words and accept that she had a valid point. No, he didn't want more kids, let alone to start over with a newborn. Dakota had had colic. The very thought of a repeat was a frightening concept.

He needed time alone to think and he wouldn't be finding it today. Forcing the uncomfortable thoughts she'd brought up to the back of his mind, he went to join everyone and try and enjoy the rest of the afternoon.

He found everyone gathered in the kitchen, obviously ready to sing "Happy Birthday" to his brother, but Fallon was nowhere to be found.

He walked over to Liam. "Did you see where Fallon went?"

"Lost your girlfriend already?"

Noah rolled his eyes.

"Okay, okay. She excused herself to go to the ladies' room." Except he'd been in the hallway where the bathroom was located. At least the one guests tended to use. And he hadn't seen her.

Was it a leap to wonder if she'd overheard his mother's comments?

He walked out of the kitchen and opened the front door where he found Fallon standing on the wraparound porch, looking out at the trees that surrounded the property. The fact that she'd walked out on the party inside left him with no doubt.

She'd heard his talk with his mother and she was obviously upset.

FALLON HADN'T MEANT to eavesdrop on Noah and his mother but she'd rounded the corner to the hallway where the bathroom was located and she'd heard her name. Stopping so she didn't interrupt, she'd paused and caught the gist of the conversation. It was the second time she'd heard that Noah didn't want more kids. For the last couple of weeks she'd been able to push the possibility from her mind and let her current reality occupy her thoughts.

But now she was faced with the truth. No longer a *what if* Noah didn't want children, he definitely did not. What did that mean for their future?

"Fallon?"

She turned at the sound of her name. "Hi, Noah." There was no avoiding this conversation, no matter how much she'd rather keep pushing it off. But talking at his parents' house during his brother's birthday party wasn't the right thing to do.

He walked over, hands in the front pockets of his dark jeans. "I know you heard my conversation with my mother."

Way to go right for the jugular, she thought. "I

didn't mean to. I heard my name... and—"

"It's okay."

"It is," she whispered, the lump in her throat growing bigger and more painful. She wanted to make this easier for him because they were both entitled to their feelings. "It's not your fault how you feel any more than it's mine that your mother is right."

"We need to talk about this," he said.

"Do we? Is there anything either of us can say to change the fact that your mother was right? You mentioned it earlier in passing and I knew then there would come a time for this." She gestured between them.

He remained silent and she understood. What could he say?

She forced herself to swallow, though it hurt so badly. "I'm going to walk back inside, say goodbye, and tell your family I'm not feeling well. Then I'll call an Uber and go home. I really need to be alone."

The tortured look on his face ripped her apart inside but she couldn't change things. Couldn't fix what was broken between them.

"Don't go."

He reached for her and she stepped back, another bid at not making things harder than they had to be.

"Okay then, at least don't go home alone. I'll take you and—"

She shook her head. "The girls might want to go with us and I'm…" She blinked back tears. "I'm not up to it right now. But no matter what, I promise I won't just disappear from their lives. We'll figure out a way to make this easier for them." Even if her heart was ripped to shreds.

With everything in her she wanted to give up her dreams of having babies and say Noah and his girls were enough for her. But she'd grown up in a big family. Big holidays, big brothers, and for herself? Big dreams.

"You're killing me, sweetheart," he said, his hands dangling uselessly at his sides.

She forced a smile. "I don't mean to. I'm trying to do just the opposite. Besides, you have to admit I'm right. So let's just get this over with, okay?" She started to walk past him and he spun her around, pulling her into his arms and pressing his lips hard against hers.

She melted against him, giving in to the power of their emotions and need. Her tongue swirled against his and she let the kiss go on long enough she'd feel the pain of leaving him even more intensely later. When she was alone.

Breaking things off, she stepped back, looking into his eyes, seeing the heartbreak she was experiencing mirrored back at her. "I love you, Noah. And I wish things were different." He reached for her hand but she turned before he could reply and headed inside to say her goodbyes.

She only wished they weren't for good, but there was no crossing this bridge without each of them giving up something that they felt deep in their core.

Chapter Twenty-Two

WHAT THE FUCK just happened? One minute Noah and Fallon were having a great day and the next? His mother blew up their relationship and it appeared to be for good.

He'd asked Charlie if she could take the girls home so he could drive Fallon but she had to leave soon for a Zoom call with her team, and she needed the time without distraction. He understood. She'd had the girls to herself for the entire week.

So he waited outside for the Uber, silence reigning between them. And when she climbed into the car and he shut her inside, his world felt dark around him.

He walked back inside, joining his family, feeling the weight of his mother's stare, but he had no desire to have another conversation. The girls' chatter distracted him, as did the opening of gifts. He wished Fallon had been there to see his brother's reaction to her candles. He'd loved the present, getting a good laugh out of all the various drink scents.

Charlie was getting ready to leave and once she'd said her goodbyes, Liam grasped him by the shoulder and propelled him out of the room and into their dad's study, shutting the door behind him.

"Have a seat and talk to me. Your mood did a one-eighty after Fallon left and I didn't buy her *I don't feel well* excuse." Since Liam had gotten to know Fallon recently, Noah wasn't surprised his brother had picked up on something being wrong.

He lowered himself into his father's favorite chair and Liam took the seat beside him. It was the chair the boys took when they'd gotten into trouble.

"What happened?" his brother asked.

"Mom happened," Noah muttered, drumming his fingers on the heavy leather of the armrest. "She cornered me in the hall and started grilling me about how Fallon was so much younger than me and would want babies one day. And how I'd already decided I was finished with the two I have, and why let us get in deeper and then have to end things?"

Nodding, Liam let out a low whistle. "Heavy. Okay, and you took this to Fallon today?"

"Hell, no. She was on her way to the bathroom when she heard her name and ended up catching the entire conversation."

"Shit." He leaned forward, his lips pulled into a firm line as he gave the situation some thought.

"Let me ask you something," Liam said. "When did you decide no more kids?"

Noah scrubbed a hand over his face. "In the middle of the night when Dakota was screaming. Colic," he reminded his brother.

"And do you mean it today? If it means losing Fallon? Or is it a mantra you've been repeating to yourself for years because you've been alone and there's been no reason to consider more children in your future?"

Noah blinked. There were times Liam was a jokester and a charmer, but he was deeper than people realized after being jilted by his fiancée three years ago. His views on his own personal relationships these days might be skewed by that incident, but he'd hit on something Noah wouldn't have thought of on his own.

"How do you feel about this woman?"

"I love her," he immediately said. "And she loves me."

Her words had settled inside him and warmed the parts of him that had been cold. For so long he'd been the twins' dad. Someone's boss. An attorney. But he hadn't been a man with his own needs. Not until Fallon had he allowed himself to think about what he wanted or deserved in this life. Put himself first for once. Not at the girls' expense. Never that. But he thought of himself, too.

"And if she got pregnant by accident, how would you feel?"

He let out a laugh. "You mean other than

shocked?"

"Yes, asshole." Liam smirked.

He closed his eyes and gave the question serious thought. Fallon pregnant with his child, her belly big and round with their baby. When Charlie had been pregnant, things were more clinical. He hadn't been in love with her but he had been enamored with the idea of being a dad. But with Fallon, he'd be hands-on. Hands on her swollen stomach, the proprietary way he'd feel looking at her.

Was it worth the potential repeat of a screaming, colicky baby? The fear of being up at night with a sick child, croup or the flu taking down the whole house? Watching first steps, first words, having someone he loved to share the experience with.

He looked at his brother, the room and his sibling coming back into focus.

"Well?"

He tipped his head back and stared at the ceiling. "I'd feel damned lucky," he admitted, the burden of his choice falling from his shoulders.

Yet he'd let her leave. He'd watched her drive away, accepting old decisions and feelings as how he felt now without giving the future and its ripe possibilities any thought. She was alone, sad, mourning the end of their relationship and he'd almost done the same.

"I hate giving you credit for anything, but thank you," he said to Liam. "I have to go talk to her."

His brother grinned. "I'm happy to take the girls home."

The door pushed open and Dylan walked inside. "Daddy, I don't feel well. My stomach hurts." She was holding on to her belly and she didn't look well at all, her pallor a slight gray.

He rose to his feet. "Did you overeat Grandma's cookies? And have too much birthday cake?"

She shook her head. "I wasn't hungry for cake. And I only had a couple of cookies."

Placing the back of his hand on her forehead, he frowned. "You feel warm. Come on. Let's get you home so you can rest. Go tell your sister we need to leave. I'll be right there."

He turned to his sibling. "Thanks, Liam. I owe you. When you find the right woman, I'll be there."

His brother's eyes widened in mock horror. Or was it real? "So many women, so little time, bro. Settling down isn't for me."

Noah shook his head, knowing Liam's carefree attitude about women was a result of that painful breakup with his ex. "For now, Liam. For now."

He spent the next twenty-four hours taking care of Dylan who'd ended up with a stomach virus. And for the twenty-four hours after that, it was Dakota's turn.

Noah was spared, as were the adults who'd been around them at his parents' house, thank goodness.

Though he'd wanted to get in touch with Fallon, the twins kept him completely busy, either taking care of them when they were sick, changing sheets, or laying beside them when they didn't feel well. As much as he'd love to reach out, anything he had to say to Fallon needed to be done in person.

WITHOUT THE GALLERY to use for her painting, Fallon holed up in the second bedroom of her house and buried herself in her dark mood, from her music choice to her artwork. She ignored her phone, both calls and texts, wanting nothing more than to be alone. Once she worked the pain out of her system, she'd show her face again but she wasn't ready.

The frustration she felt at being stuck by her needs and Noah's desires was overwhelming. She was as irrationally angry at him for being uncompromising as she was with herself. And the fact that the majority of the calls and texts she avoided had been from Brooke and nothing from Noah didn't help.

Her phone rang and a message came in from Brooke. *I'm outside your door. Open it or I'm using my key.*

"Fine!" She put down her brush and wiped her

hands on a rag before walking through her apartment and opening the door. "Come in."

"I will, grump. What's going on? Why are you avoiding me? And your dad? And your brothers? Everyone is asking me what's wrong with you and I haven't a clue."

Fallon sighed and gestured for Brooke to follow her to the kitchen. "Want something to eat or drink?" she asked.

Brooke shook her head. "No. I want answers. I'm worried about you."

No sooner had she started to speak than the tears began to flow. Somehow, she managed to repeat the story from Sunday, how she'd walked away from Noah and the girls, and she hadn't heard from him since.

"Oh, honey. Why didn't you answer? I would have been here and helped you through it."

She sniffed and grabbed the box of tissues she kept on the counter. "I wanted to suffer." After blowing her nose, she tossed the tissues in the trash and washed her hands. "Seriously, I just wanted to wallow."

Brooke slung an arm over her shoulders. "Have you eaten anything?"

Fallon shook her head. "Not much. Some crackers."

"It's ice cream time then." Brooke opened the

freezer and pulled out two pints of ice cream. "Vanilla or cookie dough?" she asked.

Thinking of how she and Noah shared a love of vanilla, she chose the cookie dough. Would avoiding his favorite flavor help make a healthy break? She had no idea.

A few minutes later, she and Brooke were curled into the family room couch, each taking an end and sharing a blanket over their feet while eating ice cream out of the containers. They didn't talk. There was nothing to say that could change how Fallon was feeling, no suggestion that would let her and Noah meet halfway.

But she was happy to have company, glad her best friend pushed past the barrier she'd erected to the outside world and forced herself in.

At least she felt less alone.

The doorbell to her apartment rang and she glanced at Brooke.

"Expecting anyone?" her friend asked.

Fallon shook her head. "Make them go away," she muttered.

"As you wish." Brooke placed her pint on the cocktail table, put the spoon inside, and rose, walking to the door.

Fallon heard muffled voices and then Brooke called out to her. "I think you're going to want to see this person."

"I don't want to see anyone," she reiterated. Couldn't a girl wallow in peace, she wondered.

Brooke's footsteps sounded as she walked back, as did someone with a heavier tread.

"I said no company!" Fallon called out.

"Not even me?" Noah asked.

She jumped in her seat. Brooke immediately walked over and took her ice cream and spoon. Then she picked up her container in the other hand. "I think my job here is done. If he's not here to patch things up, call me. I'll tell Remy to shoot his ass," she said of Fallon's former detective brother who owned a gun.

"Ouch," Noah muttered.

Brooke walked away from them and into the kitchen. Fallon listened to the sounds of her friend cleaning up, putting the ice cream in the freezer, before the front door shut behind her with a loud sound.

Noah stared at her and she returned the favor, taking in his mussed hair, the dark circles under his eyes, and the exhaustion prevalent on his face. But he was no less handsome because of it.

At least he hadn't been any happier than her. "I'm tired, Noah. If you're here to talk and rehash the impossible, I'm not up to it."

He shook his head. "I'm not up to it, either. No sooner had you left my parents' house than Dylan came down with a stomach bug. Twenty-four hours later, Dakota had it. It's been a hellish forty-eight hours."

She winced, feeling badly for him. "Are they okay now?"

He nodded. "Back to their bouncy selves. Me? Not so much."

With a sigh, she gestured toward the sofa. "Why don't you sit down?" He clearly wasn't going to leave without saying what he came to say and he looked about to fall asleep where he stood.

He chose a chair across from the couch. "How are you?" he asked.

She shook her head. "I'd think that was obvious by looking at me. Please just have your say and go. I can't do this again." It hurt too much.

"Fine. Every once in a while, Liam has something intelligent to offer to the world."

Unable not to, she laughed at his comment. "And what brilliance came out of his mouth besides what a catch he is?"

"To begin with, he asked how I felt about you and that was a no-brainer. I love you, too," he said in a gruff, sexy voice. "And I've never said that to a woman I've been involved with. Ever."

His gaze remained locked with hers as he spoke and she wasn't sure if the words were welcome.

Because she had even more to grieve now that she knew he felt the same way.

"Then he asked me how I'd feel if you came to me and said you were pregnant."

She stilled, sensing a shift in energy in the room. A shift in Noah. "What did you say?" The question came out more a whisper tinged with hope.

"That I'd feel damn lucky if you were carrying my child. He made me think and realize the thought of having a baby is way different than actually having a child with *you*."

"Which means?" She leaned in.

"Come here."

She rose from her seat and stepped closer. When she reached him, he grasped her around the waist and pulled her onto his lap.

She fell willingly, breathing in his familiar scent and wrapping her arms around his neck, hoping she wasn't in for another fall.

"It means I love you, Fallon, and I'm not letting you go. You want kids? Then I want babies. With you."

She blinked, stunned by his one-eighty. "Are you going to resent me when—"

"Never. I meant it when I said I'd be damned lucky if you got pregnant with my child."

"I didn't mean right away," she clarified. She had

business goals too. But the personal ones? They dictated who she spent the rest of her life with. And she was still unable to believe this change was real. That he was here saying everything she'd needed to hear.

He let out a low chuckle. "Coming on the heels of the massive stomach virus outbreak, I'm glad to hear that."

"So you really want a bigger family with me?"

"I want you and everything that goes along with you. If I haven't been clear, I adore you, Fallon Sterling, and I want forever with you."

Her heart rate picked up speed, happiness filling all the empty spaces inside her. "And I want forever with you. And your precious girls. I know you're a package deal."

He threaded his fingers through hers. "Do you have any idea how happy they're going to be?"

She grinned. "I have an idea. But if you want to slow things down, give them time to get used to the idea of us…"

He shook his head. "Not a chance. Now that we're on the same page about everything, it's full steam ahead." He brushed a strand of hair off her shoulder and leaned in, pressing his cheek to hers. "I love you and I'm sorry I put you through two days of hell before I got here to tell you." His warm breath fanned her ear.

"Kiss me and I'll forgive you," she whispered back.

He sat back, then braced his palms against her cheeks. "You were a temptation from the day I met you and I never thought we were meant to be but we are."

He brought their lips together in the sweetest kiss that quickly turned hot and out of control. She moaned and wriggled in his lap, feeling the hard ridge of his cock when she felt a vibration against her thigh. "What in the world?"

"My phone."

He shifted in the seat and pulled his cell from his front pocket, checking the messages. "Dakota wants me to bring home pizza for dinner."

He texted her back and placed the phone on the end table.

"Wait. I didn't think the girls had cell phones?" Fallon asked.

"It's a new development. Charlie got them phones so they could call her whenever they want. I have to admit, it comes in handy."

"What did you tell her?"

"That I was bringing home pizza and a permanent surprise."

She blinked and blinked again. "Permanent?"

He nodded. "You're moving in with us. Now that

245

I really have you, I don't want you out of my sight."

She shook her head. This man. "Ask me."

"Tell me you'll move in with me." He chuckled, then winked at her. "Will you move in with us? Wake up to the shrieking of two nine-year-olds and deal with Dakota's weird and often gross facts."

She braced her hands on his shoulders and met his gaze. "Yes, Noah. I will."

They had the rest of their lives to plan and live out their forever.

Epilogue One

Six Months Later

FALLON WALKED AROUND the gallery which was due to open in five minutes, feeling a sense of pride at the changes that had taken place. The reopening was a major event, covered by the news media thanks to a publicist they'd hired. Inside, it was just a few people, but a crowd had gathered outside, waiting.

Needing a few moments to breathe, Fallon walked into the larger back offices they'd put in during the renovation. After Clara recovered from the poisoning, she'd decided to take more time off and made Fallon a partner in the business. Fallon had wanted to buy in but Clara made it clear, Fallon was the daughter she'd never had. Her only child, with her son in prison for trying to kill them both.

To the twins, she was Aunt Clara, the older woman not wanting to seem as if she were usurping Noah's parents' place. Essentially, she became part of their family.

Noah walked into the room and wrapped his arms around her waist. "Are you ready?"

She inhaled, breathing in his sandalwood scent,

familiar and calming. She nodded. "It feels like it's been forever when in reality it's only been six months since the fire."

"It's exciting that Clara was able to buy the entire piece of real estate on this corner and expand the gallery and paint 'n' sip," he said.

"It is exciting. We also have new employees to accommodate the larger business and many more up-and-coming artists." Fallon and Clara were going to be overseers now, managers, and less hands-on. "And a fully staffed coffee bar. I can't wait to see the patron response!"

"I know you're consumed with the opening but I was hoping I could have your attention for a few minutes before the doors open."

"Of course! You can have my attention any time."

Since their newfound understanding, many changes had occurred. Fallon and Noah had sat down with the girls and discussed her moving in.

Their excitement knew no bounds and Noah had to call Charlie and wake her up to discuss the situation with her before the girls spilled the beans. As he'd told Fallon later, it was a good thing the girls' mother hadn't had an issue, since he'd blurted out his insistence that Fallon move in before running it by her.

Fallon met Noah's gaze. "What's up?" she asked, just as he dropped to one knee, pulled a small box from his pocket with one hand, and popped it open. "Fallon Sterling, will you do me the extreme honor of becoming my wife?"

"And our stepmom!" The girls, who she hadn't noticed, came rushing up beside their father.

"Oh my God, Noah." She took in the large, emerald-shaped diamond ring that stood out in a white gold setting. "This stone reminds me of my mother's." The happiness she felt having something similar to her beloved mother's ring filled her up.

"That's because it is hers. When I asked your father, he offered me her ring. And knowing how much you miss her, I couldn't think of anything better. Now can you answer me before my knee goes out?"

"Noah, yes! Yes!" He rose and pressed a long kiss to her lips. When they broke apart, she focused on the girls. "I'm so honored to become your stepmom." But she'd never try to take Charlie's place and she hoped everyone, including their mother, knew that.

"Can we call you Momma Fallon?" Dylan asked.

"We wanted to say Mommy Fallon but Grandma said we'd outgrow saying Mommy and then what would we do?" Dakota said, quoting her more practical sister.

"I love you girls. You can call me whatever makes you comfortable and happy." Her heart filled even more, threatening to overflow with pure, undiluted joy.

Clara joined them and wished them all the best. "Now, it's time to open!"

Noah slipped the ring on her finger. He grasped her hand, taking Dylan's in his free one while she grasped Dakota's in hers. And as a family, they walked into the gallery to celebrate so many things.

Epilogue Two

Another Six Months Later

NOAH WAITED FOR Fallon to walk down the aisle escorted by her father. As he stood and looked over the crowd of family and close friends, he thought over the last year of his life, which had turned out better than he could have hoped for. The twins had adjusted to Fallon moving in easily and she'd stepped into the role of stepmom like a champ. She didn't let them get away with their shenanigans but had a special way of dealing with them to avoid anger, tantrums or tears. Sometimes. They were kids, after all.

And it meant everything to him to fall asleep with her in his arms at night and wake up beside her in the morning. Now they'd make it legal before heading to Aruba for their honeymoon. The girls waited inside, dressed in light blue dresses, looking too old for his liking and utterly beautiful. Along with Brooke, they were Fallon's maids of honor. Though she could have made them junior bridesmaids, she said she'd wanted to give them starring roles to show how important they were to her.

The music started and the processional began. Noah fidgeted in anticipation, appreciating those in the wedding party, especially his daughters who walked down side by side. No giggling, they were little ladies and he couldn't be more proud.

They stood close by him, and the bridesmaids and groomsmen stood in a line on either side. Finally, the "Wedding March" began and the curtains at the end of the aisle parted. Fallon appeared, her arm hooked around her father's, and they started down the aisle.

She took his breath away in a stunning, strapless gown fitted to her lithe body. One look at her and all he wanted was to say *I do,* drag her into a private room, and ravage his wife.

He made it through the ceremony, speaking over the lump in his throat. He was touched by the sheen of tears in her eyes as he slipped the diamond band onto her finger beside her mother's stone.

They were declared husband and wife and he pulled her into his arms, dipped her low, and kissed his bride. Hand in hand, they walked up the aisle to the cheers and whistles of their guests. A few short minutes later and he had her alone in the bridal room and pulled her into his arms.

"Congratulations, Mrs. Powers."

She smiled, beaming, her face flushed. "Congratulations to you, Mr. Powers."

"I thought the ceremony would never end. Now

that you're mine, I can breathe."

Smiling, she wrapped her arms around his neck and looked into his eyes. "I have a surprise for you."

"Is it a string bikini for the honeymoon?"

She laughed at his comment. "I have one of those, yes, but that isn't it." She stepped out of his embrace and walked over to the small, white pearl purse on the counter. "I hope it's a good surprise even if it is an unplanned one."

He narrowed his gaze, wondering what she had for him. "I will love anything you give me, sweetheart. You know that."

She turned back to him, her throat moving as she visibly swallowed hard. "I hope so," she whispered, holding up a white stick. Turning it toward him, a plus sign was visible. "Surprise! I'm pregnant."

He heard the hesitancy in her tone, the slightly fearful hitch to her voice. Still, he took a second to process the news, then grinned. "Seriously?"

"I wouldn't joke about this. Please tell me you're happy."

He lowered himself to one knee, leaned forward, and pressed a kiss to her still flat belly. "I don't know how it happened but I told you I'd be lucky as hell if you were pregnant and I meant it, Fallon. I love you."

Rising, he glanced at her face. Large crocodile tears had formed in her eyes. "Really?"

"Truly."

"Remember when I had strep?"

"How could I forget? It ran rampant throughout the house." And all four of them had come down with the infection.

She nodded. "The antibiotic affected the pill I take and, to be honest, we were so busy, it never dawned on me. I know we said we'd wait but—"

"But we're having a baby. It's great news," he assured her, pressing his mouth to hers. "Let's go share the news!" He braced, bent at the knees, and lifted her into his arms, carrying her out of the bridal room and into the cocktail hour.

"We're having a baby!" he yelled out and they spent the next half hour accepting congratulations and listening to the twins argue about what roles they'd each step up and help with.

FALLON WAS DIZZY from the whirlwind events of the day. Between finding out she was pregnant this morning, getting married, and dancing the night away, she was ready to collapse. She stood by their small table of four with sweetheart chairs for Noah and Fallon, and regular ones for the twins. Of course, they popped into the oversize chairs with large fan-style backs every chance they got.

Noah strode up to her and wrapped an arm around her waist. "Hi," he said, speaking in her ear to be heard over the band.

"Hi, yourself."

"Check it out," Noah said, tipping his head toward the bar in the back of the room.

She scanned the dance floor, watching the twins dance with her father and Noah's parents, her gaze landing on the bar. The area was empty but for her brother Jared and Charlie.

He handed her a drink, picked up his glass, and together they walked toward a secluded corner of the room, their heads together as they spoke.

"Well, that's interesting," she said, smiling at the sight. "I wouldn't have thought they were each other's type. Who knew?"

"She's headed back for another four to six months," he reminded Fallon. Charlie, who'd been happy for them, had flown in for the wedding.

She nodded. "I don't think Jared's looking for anything serious. Though he's the quieter one. I don't know what he really wants." With a shrug, she said, "As long as they enjoy each other's company, I'm happy for them."

"And it's none of our business."

"But it is fun to speculate."

She turned toward him. "I'm ready to go up to our hotel room." They'd reserved the bridal suite for the night before they left tomorrow. The twins would be staying with Noah's parents while they were away since Charlie would be returning to her dig in Egypt.

He placed a proprietary hand over her stomach, something he'd been doing all night. "I can't wait to peel you out of this dress," he said in a husky voice.

"Then what are we waiting for?"

After saying quick good nights, Noah picked her up—again—and carried her across the threshold of the suite where he did, indeed, strip her out of the dress and make love to her all night long.

Thanks for reading! Next up: Jared Sterling has a one night stand with Charlie Kendall, the twins' mom. Oops! She did it again!

Read JUST ONE MORE AFFAIR

A one night stand, surprise baby, forced proximity, second chance romance!

JUST ONE MORE AFFAIR

Oops, she did it *again*...

A one-night stand with a billionaire.
A surprise pregnancy.
Can she trust his love?
Or is the baby tying them together?

Charlotte Kendall never expected history to repeat itself after a one-night stand at a wedding. Especially since a past encounter left her co-parenting twin daughters she adores. Except this time, her baby daddy is a man she can't resist.

Billionaire Jared Sterling always gets what he wants— and he wants Charlotte Kendall. When he learns she's pregnant, he's all in. But Charlotte's past has taught this independent, single mom to guard her heart. She doubts Jared's motives and believes he's only invested for the baby.

Their chemistry is undeniable and Jared will do anything to convince Charlotte *she's* his endgame. But her life is complicated and when her brother's recklessness puts Charlotte in danger, Jared takes over, proving he's offering the love and stability she has always craved.

Now Charlotte must decide—will she keep running from the man who's offering her everything, or take a chance on love?

Read JUST ONE MORE AFFAIR

Want even more Carly books?

CARLY'S BOOKLIST by Series – visit:
https://www.carlyphillips.com/CPBooklist

Sign up for Carly's Newsletter:
https://www.carlyphillips.com/CPNewsletter

Join Carly's Corner on Facebook:
https://www.carlyphillips.com/CarlysCorner

Carly on Facebook:
https://www.carlyphillips.com/CPFanpage

Carly on Instagram:
https://www.carlyphillips.com/CPInstagram

Carly's Booklist

The Kingstons — newest series first

The Sterling Family
Book 1: Just One More Moment (Remington Sterling & Raven Walsh)

Book 2: Just One More Dare (Dex Kingston & Samantha Dare)

Book 3: Just One More Mistletoe (Max Corbin & Brandy Bloom)

Book 4: Just One More Temptation (Noah Powers & Fallon Sterling)

Book 5: Just One More Affair (Charlotte Kendall & Jared Sterling)

The Kingston Family
Book 1: Just One Night (Linc Kingston & Jordan Greene)

Book 2: Just One Scandal (Chloe Kingston & Beck Daniels)

Book 3: Just One Chance (Xander Kingston & Sasha Keaton)

Book 4: Just One Spark (Dash Kingston & Cassidy Forrester)

Novella: Just Another Spark (Dash Kingston & Cassidy Forrester)

Book 5: Just One Wish (Axel Forrester)

Book 6: Just One Dare (Aurora Kingston & Nick Dare)

Book 7: Just One Kiss (Knox Sinclair & Jade Dare)

Book 8: Just One Taste (Asher Dare & Nicolette Bettencourt)

Book 9: Just One Fling (Harrison Dare & Winter Capwell)

Book 10: Just One Tease (Zach Dare & Hadley Stevens)

Book 10.5: Just One Summer (Maddox James & Gabriella Davenport)

The Dares — newest series first

Dare Nation

Book 1: Dare to Resist (Austin & Quinn)

Book 2: Dare to Tempt (Damon & Evie)

Book 3: Dare to Play (Jaxon & Macy)

Book 4: Dare to Stay (Brandon & Willow)

Novella: Dare to Tease (Hudson & Brianne)

* Paul Dare's sperm donor kids

The Sexy Series

Book 1: More Than Sexy (Jason Dare & Faith)

Book 2: Twice As Sexy (Tanner & Scarlett)

Book 3: Better Than Sexy (Landon & Vivienne)

Novella: Sexy Love (Shane & Amber)

The Knight Brothers
Book 1: Take Me Again (Sebastian & Ashley)
Book 2: Take Me Down (Parker & Emily)
Book 3: Dare Me Tonight (Ethan Knight & Sienna Dare)
Novella: Take The Bride (Sierra & Ryder)
Take Me Now – Short Story (Harper & Matt)

NY Dares Series (NY Dare Cousins)
Book 1: Dare to Surrender (Gabe & Isabelle)
Book 2: Dare to Submit (Decklan & Amanda)
Book 3: Dare to Seduce (Max & Lucy)

Dare to Love Series
Book 1: Dare to Love (Ian & Riley)
Book 2: Dare to Desire (Alex & Madison)
Book 3: Dare to Touch (Dylan & Olivia)
Book 4: Dare to Hold (Scott & Meg)
Book 5: Dare to Rock (Avery & Grey)
Book 6: Dare to Take (Tyler & Ella)
A Very Dare Christmas – Short Story (Ian & Riley)

* Sienna Dare gets together with Ethan Knight in **The Knight Brothers** (Dare Me Tonight).

* Jason Dare gets together with Faith in the **Sexy Series** (More Than Sexy).

For the most recent Carly books, visit CARLY'S
BOOKLIST page
www.carlyphillips.com/CPBooklist

Other Indie Series — newest series first

Hot Heroes Series
Book 1: Touch You Now (Kane & Halley)
Book 2: Hold You Now (Jake & Phoebe)
Book 3: Need You Now (Braden & Juliette)
Book 4: Want You Now (Kyle & Andi)

Bodyguard Bad Boys
Book 1: Rock Me (Ben & Summer)
Book 2: Tempt Me (Austin & Mia)
Novella: His To Protect (Shane & Talia)

Billionaire Bad Boys
Book 1: Going Down Easy (Kaden & Lexie)
Book 2: Going Down Fast (Lucas & Maxie)
Book 3: Going Down Hard (Derek & Cassie)
Book 4: Going In Deep (Julian & Kendall)
Going Down Again – Short Story (Kaden & Lexie)

For the most recent Carly books, visit CARLY'S
BOOKLIST page
www.carlyphillips.com/CPBooklist

Carly's Originally Traditionally Published Books

Serendipity's Finest Series
Book 1: Perfect Fit (Mike & Cara)
Book 2: Perfect Fling (Cole & Erin)
Book 3: Perfect Together (Sam & Nicole)
Book 4: Perfect Strangers (Luke & Alexa)

Serendipity Series
Book 1: Serendipity (Ethan & Faith)
Book 2: Kismet (Trevor & Lissa)
Book 3: Destiny (Nash & Kelly)
Book 4: Fated (Nick & Kate)
Book 5: Karma (Dare & Liza)

Costas Sisters
Book 1: Under the Boardwalk (Quinn & Ariana)
Book 2: Summer of Love (Ryan & Zoe)

Ty and Hunter
Book 1: Cross My Heart (Ty & Lilly)
Book 2: Sealed with a Kiss (Hunter & Molly)

The Lucky Series
Book 1: Lucky Charm (Derek & Gabrielle)
Book 2: Lucky Streak (Mike & Amber)
Book 3: Lucky Break (Jason & Lauren)

The Most Eligible Bachelor Series
Book 1: Kiss Me if You Can (Sam & Lexie)
Book 2: Love Me If You Dare (Rafe & Sara)

The Hot Zone
Book 1: Hot Stuff (Brandon & Annabelle)
Book 2: Hot Number (Damian & Micki)
Book 3: Hot Item (Riley & Sophie)
Book 4: Hot Property (John & Amy)

The Chandler Brothers
Book 1: The Bachelor (Roman & Charlotte)
Book 2: The Playboy (Rick & Kendall)
Book 3: The Heartbreaker (Chase & Sloane)

The Simply Series
Book 1: Simply Sinful (Kane & Kayla)
Book 2: Simply Scandalous (Logan & Catherine)
Book 3: Simply Sensual (Ben & Gracie)
Book 4: Body Heat (Jake & Brianne)
Book 5: Simply Sexy (Colin & Rina)

Carly Classics
Book 1: The Right Choice (Mike & Carly)
Book 2: Perfect Partners (Griffin & Chelsie)
Book 3: Unexpected Chances (Dylan & Holly)
Book 4: Worthy of Love (Kevin & Nikki)

For the most recent Carly books, visit CARLY'S
BOOKLIST page
www.carlyphillips.com/CPBooklist

Carly's Still Traditionally Published Books

Stand-Alone Books

Brazen

Secret Fantasy

Seduce Me

The Seduction

More Than Words Volume 7 – Compassion Can't Wait

Naughty Under the Mistletoe

Grey's Anatomy 101 Essay

For the most recent Carly books, visit CARLY'S BOOKLIST page

www.carlyphillips.com/CPBooklist

About the Author

NY Times, Wall Street Journal, and USA Today Bestseller, Carly Phillips is the queen of Alpha Heroes, at least according to The Harlequin Junkie Reviewer. Carly married her college sweetheart and lives in Purchase, NY along with her crazy dogs who are featured on her Facebook and Instagram pages. The author of over 75 romance novels, she has raised two incredible daughters and is now an empty nester. Carly's book, The Bachelor, was chosen by Kelly Ripa as her first romance club pick. Carly loves social media and interacting with her readers. Want to keep up with Carly? Sign up for her newsletter and receive TWO FREE books at www.carlyphillips.com.

Made in the USA
Columbia, SC
03 February 2025